*Just like the townsfolk said,
Nora Darby was prickly, all right,*

Stephen thought. But maybe he needed a good challenge in his life. Imagining Nora yielding to him, hissing even as she purred, stirred his blood.

"I'd like to see you again," he said.

Nora looked at him as if he'd suddenly sprouted purple horns and a tail. "I don't *date.*" The word was laced with contempt.

"Why not?"

She opened her mouth, then closed it again. Finally she simply hurried toward the door.

Stephen watched her go. He wasn't looking for the love of his life. He'd had that once and lost her. Sassy Nora Darby wasn't looking for anything permanent, either. But maybe the[y] to help each other.

Because if she didn[']t to do...other things.

And watching her m[o] would probably do those oth[er] very, very well....

Dear Reader,

Though each Special Edition novel is sprinkled with magic, you should know that the authors of your favorite romances are *not* magicians—they're women just like you.

"Romance is a refuge for me. It lifts my spirits." Sound familiar? That's Christine Rimmer's answer to why she reads—and writes—romance. Christine is the author of this month's *The Tycoon's Instant Daughter,* which launches our newest in-line continuity the STOCKWELLS OF TEXAS. Like you, she started out as a reader while she had a multifaceted career—actress, janitor, waitress, phone sales representative. "But I really wanted one job where I wouldn't have to work any other jobs," Christine recalls. Now, thirteen years and thirty-seven books later, Ms. Rimmer is an established voice in Special Edition.

Some other wonderful voices appear this month. Susan Mallery delivers *Unexpectedly Expecting!,* the latest in her LONE STAR CANYON series. Penny Richards's juicy series RUMOR HAS IT... continues with *Judging Justine.* It's love Italian-style with Tracy Sinclair's *Pretend Engagement,* an alluring romance set in Venice. The cat is out of the bag, so to speak, in Diana Whitney's *The Not-So-Secret Baby.* And young Trent Brody is hoping to see his *Beloved Bachelor Dad* happily married in Crystal Green's debut novel.

We aim to give you six novels every month that lift *your* spirits. Tell me what you like about Special Edition. What would you like to see more of in the line? Write to: Silhouette Books, 300 East 42nd St., 6th Floor, New York, NY 10017. I encourage you to be part of making your favorite line even better!

Best,

Karen Taylor Richman
Senior Editor

Unexpectedly Expecting!

SUSAN MALLERY

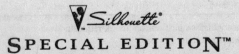

Silhouette®

SPECIAL EDITION™

Published by Silhouette Books

America's Publisher of Contemporary Romance

To Maureen Child, a gifted writer and a great friend. Your wit, charm and general mouthiness were the inspiration for Nora Darby. Kinda scary, huh?

 SILHOUETTE BOOKS

ISBN 0-373-24370-7

UNEXPECTEDLY EXPECTING!

Copyright © 2001 by Susan Macias Redmond

Visit Silhouette at www.eHarlequin.com

Printed in U.S.A.

Books by Susan Mallery

SUSAN MALLERY

is the bestselling author of over thirty-five books for Silhouette. Always a fan of romance novels, Susan finds herself in the unique position of living out her own personal romantic fantasy with the new man in her life. Susan lives in the state of Washington with her handsome hero husband and her two adorable-but-not-bright cats.

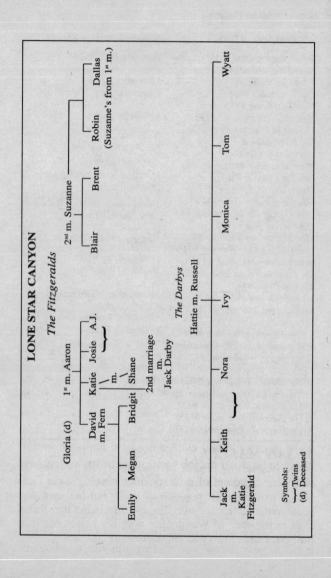

LONE STAR CANYON

The Fitzgeralds

Gloria (d)

1ˢᵗ m. Aaron

2ⁿᵈ m. Suzanne

David m. Fern — Bridgit

Katie — Josie — A.J.

Blair — Brent

Robin — Dallas
(Suzanne's from 1ˢᵗ m.)

Emily — Megan

Katie
m.
Shane

2nd marriage
m.
Jack Darby

The Darbys

Hattie m. Russell

Jack
m.
Katie Fitzgerald

Keith — Nora — Ivy — Monica — Tom — Wyatt

Symbols:
⌒ Twins
(d) Deceased

Chapter One

"Don't even think about it, Dr. Remington," Nurse Rosie warned. "Braver men than you have tried to scale that particular mountain and few of them have lived to tell the tale."

Stephen Remington glanced at his nurse and frowned. "What mountain? Texas is flat."

He knew that firsthand, Stephen thought. He'd driven across most of it when he'd moved to Lone Star Canyon from Boston six months before. Texas was big and flat and everything he'd hoped it would be when he'd left his job running an urban emergency room for the quiet of country doctoring.

His petite nurse-receptionist gave him a knowing look. "I was using a metaphor," she said with the patience of a woman long used to the frailties of the male mind. "I saw you staring out the window. It wasn't hard to figure out what...or who...had captured your attention.''

She pointed out the glass window that fronted his generous office space. Stephen followed the direction of her hand and saw that she'd assumed he was spying on his neighbors across the street.

The Lone Star Canyon Medical Offices shared the downtown area with a couple of banks, three restaurants, a sporting goods store, several clothing shops and a hair salon known as the Snip 'n Clip. The latter establishment was directly across from his office. Normally tinted windows kept out prying eyes, but today, with the afternoon so dark and the shop so bright, it was easy to see into the salon.

He could see two people clearly. One was an elderly white-haired woman in the process of getting her hair lacquered for the week. The other woman wielded the can of hair spray with great style and generosity. He guessed that she was the one Rosie had thought he was admiring.

Stephen glanced at the tall brunette wearing tight jeans, boots and a cropped red T-shirt that exposed a strip of skin that included a very neatly tucked ''inny.'' Her dark hair fell in loose, sensual curls to the middle of her back. She moved with the sexy grace of a woman who can have any man she wanted without wanting a single one.

''Her?'' he said, well aware that if he could see into her place, she could see out to his. Fortunately the woman didn't seem to notice him.

''That's the one,'' Rose said. ''Nora Darby. She might look all soft and sweet on the outside, but on the inside she's about as friendly as a gut-shot mama bear. Nora doesn't like men, and with good reason. I don't want to burst your bubble, Doctor, but better men than you have tried and failed.''

''I see.''

Looking at Nora he could understand why they'd tried. She had it all—a great body with a pretty face. If she could speak intelligently on any subject, she would be perfect. Not for him, of course, but maybe for someone else.

''I'll admit that she's very attractive,'' he told his nurse, ''but you don't have to worry. I'm not in the market for a woman—gut-shot mama bear or not. Besides, she isn't what I was looking at.''

He pointed to the dark gray-green cloud that had been hovering on the edge of the horizon. Most of it was hidden behind the building across the street, but he could see the top of it, swirling closer and closer as they talked. It was almost as if a part of the sky had reached down to—

Rosie screamed and grabbed his arm. ''Tornado,'' she yelled, and headed for the front door.

Stephen frowned. He tugged free of his nurse's insistent grip. ''What are you talking about?''

''We have to get into a storm cellar,'' she said frantically. ''Oh, supplies. There'll be injuries.'' She glanced out of the window again and shrieked. ''It's nearly here.''

As she spoke, Stephen realized that the wind had picked up around them and that there was a peculiar heaviness in the air. Tornado? He'd heard about them, of course, but he was from the East Coast where phenomena like that occurred on the evening news, not in real life.

But Rosie's panic was real enough. His normally unflappable nurse ran for the front desk and jerked the emergency first aid kit from its rack on the wall. Stephen took it from her as she grabbed his arm again and headed out the front door.

As they stepped into the street, he could hear the approaching sound of a train. Except there weren't any train tracks in Lone Star Canyon. His gaze was drawn across the street. Not toward the very tempting Ms. Nora Darby, but to her elderly clientele, all of whom were going to have trouble making it to shelter in time. He shifted course and headed toward the Snip 'n Clip.

"I love this song," Mrs. Gelson said as she admired herself in the mirror.

Nora tuned in to the sentimental song coming from the small stereo in the back of the shop.

Mrs. Gelson sighed and patted her helmet of white hair. "Makes me miss my Bill. He used to sing this to me."

Right, Nora thought as she pasted a smile on her face. This would be the same Bill who left his wife and three kids to play poker two nights a week, regardless of whether or not there was enough food in the house. The fact that the money he lost might be needed for the phone bill or shoes for the kids had never occurred to him. And Mrs. Gelson hadn't said a word in protest. The old couple had been married forty years when Bill had "gone to his reward," as Mrs. Gelson had put it. At least the bastard hadn't borrowed against his life insurance, Nora thought grimly. So although she was far from well off, his widow's last days would be better than her years with him.

But Mrs. Gelson wouldn't see it that way. Now that

Bill was gone, he was a saint and Mrs. Gelson lived to tell stories about his greatness.

"You always said your husband was a romantic," Nora said warmly, telling the lie that her client wanted to hear. Because it was kind and the right thing to do. Because most women seemed to have convenient memories where men were concerned. Not that Nora had that problem. She had an excellent memory and she never made the same mistake twice.

Mrs. Gelson handed her a ten dollar bill and waited for her two dollars change. Then she dropped one of the bills onto Nora's station, gave a wave and started for the front door.

Nora stared at the single dollar. She was never going to make any money if she didn't start raising her prices. Actually she had…several times over the past ten years. However, there were certain customers who couldn't afford more, so she didn't charge them more. There were the seniors on limited incomes. Debbie Watson, whose husband had run off, leaving her with four kids and a pile of bills. And nearly a half dozen others in similar circumstances.

"It's only money," Nora murmured philosophically as she pocketed the tip and turned to help her elderly client to the door.

Just then the front door flew open. A tall, sandy-haired man in a white jacket stalked inside. Nora recognized Stephen Remington, the town's new doctor. Successful, single, yeah, yeah, folks had been singing his praises since he'd first arrived. She was deeply unimpressed and continued to drive sixty miles to a different town with a female doctor.

She looked at him now and was pleased that despite his wide hazel eyes and lean good looks, she was immune. As always.

"We don't do men's hair here," she said sweetly. "You'll have to go to the barber shop down the street."

"What?"

She sighed. Men could be so incredibly slow, she thought, wondering how he'd made it through medical school. "I said—"

He cut her off with a quick shake of his head. "I don't care. There's a tornado coming. Everyone into the shelter."

Before Nora or anyone could react, the warning siren went off. Sound exploded through the small salon. She swore under her breath as she glanced around at the full chairs. Except for herself and the other three stylists, no one was under sixty-five. They were not a wildly mobile group and the shelter was nearly half a block away, next to the bank.

"Jill, you take Mrs. McDirmity," Nora said as she ran to the dryers and quickly raised the hoods. "Come on, we have to hurry. Tornado's coming."

As she spoke, the noise outside increased. She realized it wasn't all from the wind and the sirens. Instead there was a loud roaring, punctuated by ripping, tearing and banging, as if the world around them was being torn apart. In less than two minutes all her elderly patrons were moving toward the shelter. Dr. Remington had an arm around two ladies, one with tightly wound curlers in her hair. Dust and debris battered them, but they weren't hit by anything worse than a few small branches.

Up ahead Nurse Rosie stood at the entrance to the cellar. She hustled people down into the safety underground as quickly as possible. Jill raced by, pushing Mrs. McDirmity in her wheelchair. The doctor lowered his two ladies into the cellar, then called down for help. Together he and one of the guys from the diner across the street carried the elderly woman to safety. The wheelchair was folded up and pulled inside.

"Come on, Mrs. Gelson," Nora said as she steadied her customer. The widow took cautious steps into the underground shelter.

Nora was the last one on the street. She took a quick look around, searching for stragglers, but didn't see anyone. Her gaze lingered on familiar buildings and businesses. How much would survive the storm?

She sent up a quick prayer that there wouldn't be any deaths, then stepped into the cellar. Even as she reached for the door to pull it closed, she couldn't help pausing and looking back as the tornado swept close enough to take the roof off an abandoned building at the end of the street.

Long, tall, swirling darkness circled up to the sky. The sound was so loud as to be a vibration. The ground shook, the heavens moaned. She had once heard a tornado described as the finger of God, writing across a landscape, destroying without thought or plan. But she'd never witnessed the raw power before. It was amazing. It was—

"What the hell are you doing?" a male voice asked, just as two arms came around her midsection and jerked her into the semidarkness of the cellar.

Nora instinctively released the door. It banged shut. She sensed more than saw movement as someone reached up to bolt it securely. But what really captured her attention was the heat of the man holding her so close.

He held her in an awkward embrace—her back to his front. But that didn't stop her from feeling the warmth of his body, or his strength. She was tall, nearly five-nine but he was taller. The arms around her nestled just below her breasts. When one of his hands moved, his fingers brushed against the bare skin of her tummy. She shivered. Not from cold or fear of the approaching storm but because... well...because—

Nora pressed her lips together and shoved the arms away. She didn't know why she shivered, nor did she care. She took a step away from the man who had captured her so neatly, then turned to scowl at him.

Her gaze settled on the sandy-haired man in the white coat. He had hazel eyes, lean features and freckles. She'd heard him described as handsome, but she was immune. Stephen Remington, the town's new doctor. Of course. No one else would have dared to touch her that way.

She arched one eyebrow, a trick she'd taught herself in junior high. "I wouldn't have thought a doctor would have to resort to free feels," she said casually, expecting him to get angry and sputter a protest to her assault on his reputation.

Instead Dr. Remington, new guy in town, gave her a lazy once-over, starting at her expensive boots and heading as far north as her breasts, then ending at her exposed stomach. "I wouldn't have thought a woman your age would have to resort to dressing like a teenager just to get attention."

"You mistake my meaning," she said coolly. "I'm not interested in attention. At least not from you."

She was aware of their interested audience. In the small storm cellar everyone heard every word. Nora wished she'd kept her mouth shut. She'd been stupid enough to stand on the steps, staring at the approaching storm. The doctor had simply dragged her inside so they wouldn't all be killed.

Not knowing how else to end their conversation, she turned her back on him and checked with her elderly clients. The shelter was about twenty feet square, with benches along three of the four walls. There were enough supplies to last a couple of dozen people for two days, and a portable toilet was tucked into a curtained alcove. Everyone from the Snip 'n Clip had made it into the shelter safely. Her staff circled among their clients, offering hugs and words of comfort.

Mrs. McDirmity touched the curls of her new perm. "At least Jill had already rinsed out the solution," she said with a slight smile that trembled at the corners. "I hope my cats are going to be safe."

Nora settled next to her and took her bent fingers in her own. "You know how they love to hide under beds and sofas when they get scared," she told the older woman. "That's the best place for them right now. Instinct will keep them safe."

Mrs. McDirmity nodded. "I know. I just worry. They're all I have."

Nora talked to each of her customers, then chatted with several patrons from the diner. She was careful to avoid Dr. Remington. She often felt his gaze on her, but she didn't return the attention. As she'd told him before, she wasn't interested. Not in him or any man. She'd learned her lesson a long time ago.

The noise outside grew worse as the storm passed

overhead. Crashes and the sound of breaking glass competed with the roaring of the wind.

In the corner, Mrs. Arnold began to wheeze. She reached for her handbag, but couldn't catch her breath enough to open it and pull out her inhaler.

"Asthma," Nora told the doctor as he moved to the woman.

Stephen Remington gave her a quick nod. "I know. She's my patient."

Nora gritted her teeth. "Well, excuse me for trying to help," she muttered under her breath, and hoped the storm would be over soon. If she had to spend much more time trapped with that horrible man, fur was going to fly.

Nearly twenty minutes later, they emerged from the cellar. Nora was one of the last to step out into the murky darkness that was just beginning to clear. The main street had been spared, so her shop was still standing. But two side streets looked as if they'd been crushed by a giant. Debris lay scattered everywhere, and there was a bright red pickup truck parked on the sidewalk by the hardware store. A bright red pickup truck that hadn't been there before the storm.

The first light drops of rain fell, making her jog toward her shop. The storm was moving northeast, which meant the ranch had already been hit. She wanted to call and see if everything was all right with her family.

She caught up with a couple of her clients as everyone hurried to cover. She offered assistance in the way of a sturdy arm. As she and the last stragglers entered the salon, Jill put down the phone.

"It's dead," her stylist said. "No real surprise there. We don't have electricity, either."

Nora grinned. "I can fix one of those problems, if not the other." She walked over to her purse and pulled out her cell phone. "Welcome to the new century. If the cell towers survived we should have service this way."

She turned on the small phone, then handed it to Jill. "You've got kids. Check on them first. I'm sure they're fine, though. Judging from the direction the storm is heading, I'll bet it missed your place by several miles."

Her stylist gave her a grateful smile, then began pushing numbers. Nora saw that Mary and Kathy had already helped their clients collect purses and coats. Everyone was instructed to stay home until power was restored, then return to get the rest of their hair treatment.

Mrs. Arnold, her asthma under control and her hair still tightly rolled in curlers, slipped a scarf over her head. "This will probably dry on its own," she said cheerfully. "I'll come back when it does and you can comb it out."

"Absolutely," Nora promised. She was about to say something else when she noticed Rosie running toward the medical office across the street.

Nora stepped outside. "Are there injuries?" she yelled.

Rosie paused to catch her breath. "About a dozen or more. Orchard Park is completely gone. There were young kids at home with their moms, plus the construction workers at the new places. Dr. Remington is assessing the injuries now, and we're going to call in a helicopter for the worst ones. I need to bring supplies.''

Orchard Park was a new residential subdivision in Lone Star Canyon. It was only about half-completed with dozens of houses in various stages of construction. The homes were smaller and less expensive—perfect starter places, which meant plenty of families with young children.

''Do you need another pair of hands?'' Nora asked. ''Everyone here is fine. I don't know first aid but I can follow directions.''

Rosie gave her a grateful smile. ''Absolutely. Come help me carry stuff back, then we'll put you to work.''

Nora quickly made arrangements for the salon. Jill was going home to check on her kids. Mary would walk a couple of their clients home while Kathy stayed at the salon. That taken care of, Nora hurried toward the medical offices and prayed that the injuries were minor. For herself she also prayed that she didn't have to see too much blood. She could verbally take down any man anywhere, but the sight of blood sent her to her knees.

The helicopter lifted off with a rush of wind that reminded Stephen of the tornado. When the pilot had turned west, toward the county hospital, Stephen shifted mental gears, releasing that patient to the care of the Medi-Vac team and focusing on the few people he had left to treat. Nurse Rosie, efficient as always, had helped him evaluate injuries. She'd collected supplies, found family members and had generally acted like the professional he knew her to be. What was surprising was her assistant.

When Rosie had run back to the office for more supplies, she'd returned with an armful of necessities and Nora Darby. The beautiful twenty-something brunette didn't know squat about being a nurse, but she pitched in wherever Rosie said, applying pressure, irrigating cuts, holding hands, offering words of comfort. She'd gone pale a few times, but otherwise had been a trouper. She might have a dangerous mouth on her, but she also had plenty of backbone and compassion.

He walked to the makeshift first aid station he and Rosie had set up in the parking lot of Kroger's market. The long awning provided cover from the rain that continued to fall. Stephen checked stitches in the index finger of a sobbing four-year-old, then removed glass from a young man's eye.

"You'll need to come back in the morning," he told the carpenter. "I'll take off the patch and we'll do a quick vision test. But from what I can see, you're going to be just fine."

"Thanks, Doc."

The two men shook hands. Rosie walked over and smiled at the patient, then looked at Stephen. "We're about done here," she said. "Do you want to head back to the office in case we get walk-ins? I can stay behind and gather the equipment."

"I'll help," said one of the construction guys who had brought in his buddy. "We can put everything in my truck."

Stephen figured his generosity had less to do with an altruistic nature and more to do with Rosie's curvy, petite figure and warm brown eyes. In the past six months he'd learned that his incredibly efficient nurse was in her mid-thirties, divorced and kept to herself in her spare time. Sort of like Nora, he thought, eyeing the tall woman talking to a young mother with two scared but uninjured kids. Except Rosie always had a kind word for everyone and Nora had a chip on her shoulder the size of an SUV.

He and Rosie were about the same age. They were both single. He supposed that something should have sparked between them, but it hadn't. They were work friends, nothing more. So far no woman had captured his attention—not that he was surprised.

He left Rosie with the calf-eyed construction guy and started walking back to the center of town. From the corner of his eye, he saw Nora move in his direction, then pause as if the thought of them sharing each other's company was more than she could stand.

"I won't bite," he promised, motioning for her to join him.

She raised a single eyebrow. "I wasn't worried about you doing anything," she said in a bored tone that implied whatever he might want to do couldn't be of interest to her.

Stephen considered himself a sensible man, but for the first time in a long time he felt himself wanting to respond to a challenge. Even more fascinating, as the tall beauty fell into step next to him, he found himself intrigued by the woman. Who was Nora Darby and why did she hate every man on sight?

"Thanks for your help today," he said.

"Not a problem." She tossed her hair back over her shoulder. "We were lucky. There wasn't much damage in town. I've talked to my mom on the cellular phone and I heard that our ranch is fine, but I don't know about the others. You could get a few more injuries from the outlying areas."

He hadn't thought of that. "Good thing we're going back to the office, then," he said. "People will look for me there."

She opened her mouth to reply, but before she could say anything, a pickup truck doing at least fifty rounded the corner. The vehicle nearly went up on two wheels. The driver spotted them and started honking, then slid to a stop in the center of the road.

"Doc, Doc, you gotta help!" An old man climbed out of the cab and raced around to the bed of the truck. "My boy. He's cut real bad."

Stephen was already running toward the tailgate. He climbed up and registered that Nora had followed.

A man in his late twenties lay stretched out on several blankets. His skin was blue-white, his eyes closed, and there was blood everywhere.

Stephen heard a faint moan from beside him, but couldn't spare her a glance. "Where is he cut?" he asked.

"On the upper arm, by his shoulder," the old man said. "I put pressure on it but the blood wouldn't stop."

Stephen saw the wad of bandages and lifted them. Blood spurted. He shoved the cloths back in place. There was no way to tell how much blood the man had lost. Too much, for sure. He was already in shock.

Stephen looked at the old man. "Drive," he commanded. "We've got to get him to my office. Now!"

The father complied, hurrying to slide behind the wheel. Stephen opened the first aid kit he'd carried back and dug out several thick bandages. He replaced the soaked ones with a fresh one and ordered Nora to press down hard on the open wound.

The truck bounced through the center of town and screeched to a halt in front of the medical offices.

"Don't move," he instructed Nora as he jumped down and ran inside.

Less than a minute later he returned with two IVs—O negative blood and saline. When he had them hooked up, he traded places with Nora.

"I'm going to have to sew him up," he said, looking at her for the first time since he'd climbed in the back of the truck. She was nearly as white as his patient. "Can you help me?"

She nodded, then swallowed. "I need about thirty seconds first."

For what? he wondered. But before he could ask, she scrambled out of the truck, ran to a nearby trash can and threw up. As promised, in thirty seconds, she was back at his side.

"Are you all right?" he asked.

"No, but that doesn't matter. I'm not going to pass out and if I have to puke again, I'll do it over the side."

She pulled on the gloves he passed her, then listened while he explained the procedure. When he handed her more bandages and an irrigation solution, she gamely did as he instructed. She had to pause to throw up again, but otherwise was as calm and efficient as Nurse Rosie herself.

It was dark by the time the ambulance had pulled away to take the man to the hospital. Nora leaned against the wall of the medical office and told herself to keep breathing. At least her stomach had settled in the past couple of hours. She hadn't thrown up so much since a bout with the stomach flu three years before, and frankly she could happily go a lifetime without having it happen again.

But despite feeling weak and shaky, she was also proud. Even though her medical training consisted of knowing how to apply a Band-Aid, she'd been able to help today. She'd aided her community in its time of need.

She looked at the now-dark Snip 'n Clip and thought about going over to put everything to right in the shop. Electricity had been restored around five, so she could sweep and vacuum and... She sighed. Not tonight. She was too tired.

"How do you feel?"

She looked up and saw Stephen Remington walking toward her. He'd removed his blood-spattered coat along with his tie. Before she could answer, he touched her forehead, then reached for her wrist and took her pulse. What was more annoying than him touching her was the way her heartbeat seemed to flutter slightly at the contact. Okay, the man was a halfway decent doctor, she thought grudgingly. That didn't give him the right to examine her.

"I'm fine," she said, pulling free of his fingers and summoning a weak excuse for a glare. "Say thank you and move along."

"Thank you," he said. "But I'm not moving along. You haven't had anything to eat today, and what you ate this morning is long gone."

"In more ways than one," she said, smiling in spite of herself.

"My point exactly. So let me express my gratitude in a practical way. Let me buy you dinner." He pointed to the diner open at the end of the street.

"I've sampled most of what they have on the menu. It's not half-bad."

She planted her hands on her hips. "Thanks for sharing that but you do realize that I was born in this town and that I've lived here all my life? Chances are I've eaten at the diner more times than you, so I don't need your commentary on the menu."

"Why are you so crabby? Must be low blood sugar. You need food."

He put his hand on the small of her back and urged her forward. Amazingly enough...she let him.

Chapter Two

She had *not* been thinking, Nora thought in disgust as she and Stephen Remington were led to a booth at the rear of the Lone Star Café. Normally the diner was full for breakfast and lunch, but fairly empty for dinner. However, with half the town still not having electricity and the diner being on the "have" side, families had come in to get a home-cooked meal and to talk about the tornado. Which meant there were plenty of interested parties to watch her sit down across from the doc and to make whispered comments that just happened to drift across the entire restaurant.

She made sure she took the seat that put her back to the crowd so she wouldn't have to watch their intrigued expressions. She sighed. There wasn't much do in Lone Star Canyon *but* talk about the neighbors. Despite a couple of spectacular exceptions, she'd managed to stay out of the limelight. Tonight that had changed.

"Why the heavy sigh?" Stephen asked as he picked up a menu. But rather than studying the list of offerings, he gazed at her, as if her answer was the most interesting thing he was bound to hear all day.

"People will talk," she said shortly. She didn't have to look at the menu. She ate here enough that she could practically recite it by heart.

"About the tornado? Why not? Things like that don't happen all that often."

She was willing to admit he was reasonably good-looking and he'd worked hard to save several lives. She'd heard that he was a nice man, not that she was interested or looking, but he had to be about as thick as a board.

"Not the storm," she said, wishing Trixie would hurry and take their order, or even better, that she hadn't agreed to dinner in the first place. "About me being here with you."

"Oh."

There was a wealth of meaning in that single syllable. She wasn't sure what, but she didn't like it.

"Yes, *oh.* I don't want the entire town speculating about my personal life."

"Because…" His voice trailed off.

She leaned forward and lowered her voice. She also spoke slowly so he could understand her meaning. "Because people might think we're on a date."

"I've heard that you don't date much," he admitted. "In fact I was informed that better men than me have tried and failed in that department."

"I do not appreciate being spoken about behind my back."

"As you weren't in the room it would have been difficult to have the conversation in front of you."

"You could have not had it at all."

He held up his hands in a gesture of surrender. "I didn't start it, someone else did. I simply participated."

She pressed her lips together but didn't respond. There was no point in talking about this any further. However, Stephen didn't share her opinion.

"So what's the big deal?" he asked. "How come you don't go out much?"

"Miss Nora hates men," a voice announced cheerfully.

Nora held in a groan. Her wish for Trixie to appear had been granted, but she was sure the timing couldn't be worse.

Stephen turned his attention to the pretty forty-something waitress with big hair the color of fire. Trixie gave him a flirtatious wink.

"Nora here is our Himalayan mountain range. You can look all you want and on a clear day she seems real approachable, but if you try to conquer her, you're gonna freeze to death."

"Thank you for sharing, Trixie," Nora said dryly.

"Just trying to help," the waitress offered with a big smile. "The meat loaf is great tonight, as always. So's the fried chicken. I'd pass on the fish. It sat out a bit while the tornado ripped through town."

Stephen touched his menu. "Why don't you give us a minute. In the meantime, Nora, what would you like to drink?"

"Coffee," she said, wishing there was a way to walk out of the diner and never be heard from again. She could feel the heat flaring on her cheeks. It was like being sixteen again and confessing to a girlfriend that she had a crush on Bobby Jones. Unfortunately his little sister had been lurking around the corner and had run off to blab the news to the entire school. Nora had endured an entire week of singsong chants of "Nora loves Bobby." The fact that the object of her desire had asked her to go to homecoming with him had only taken away part of the sting.

It's not that she was interested in Stephen Remington, but she didn't appreciate being compared to a mountain range that could freeze a man to death.

"I'll have coffee, too," he said.

When Trixie left there was a moment of silence between them. Nora searched frantically for a neutral topic. Anything that didn't involve her romantic past. Unfortunately her mind was blank.

"I heard that there was some damage on several of the nearby ranches," Stephen said casually. "You mentioned you'd spoken with your family. They're fine, right?"

She was so grateful, she almost decided she liked him. *Almost.* "Yes. My mom said that except for my brother's house being totaled, the damage was minor." She thought about Jack's small two-bedroom structure. "He'll be able to rebuild fairly easily. The hands were all accounted for. She told me there was more damage at the neighboring Fitzgerald place. The fence line was knocked down, but the great patriarch Aaron won't let anyone help repair it, which is typical."

Stephen leaned forward. A lock of his sandy brown hair fell across his forehead, giving him an oddly appealing look. Innocently devious, like a little boy about to pull a prank.

"That's right. You're a Darby, aren't you? One part of the infamous Darby-Fitzgerald feud."

Trixie appeared with the coffee. Nora quickly ordered meat loaf while Stephen picked the fried chicken. When the waitress left, he shrugged. "I know food like that is bad for me, but it's a weakness. I allow myself to have it a couple of times a month. I figured I'd earned it today."

She thought about the lives he'd saved, how he'd stayed so calm, despite all the injuries. While she'd been busy barfing her guts out, he'd been fixing the problem.

He took the coffee mug in his strong-looking hands. "So tell me about the feud. Why did it start, and when? And why are the fences Aaron's responsibility? They're shared between the two families, aren't they?"

She raised her eyebrows. "You want me to squeeze a hundred and forty years of history into a five-minute recap?"

"Something like that."

She sipped her coffee, feeling the jolt of heat as it hit her stomach. Suddenly she was starving. "Explaining about the fence is a whole lot easier. The Darbys and Fitzgeralds have nearly twenty miles of shared fence. About sixty or seventy years ago the families were in court about one thing or another. They did that a lot back then. Anyway, the judge was so tired of always seeing them in his court that he broke the fence up into five-mile sections. Each family is responsible for ten miles. If they don't keep it repaired, they're fined ten percent of the previous years' income."

Stephen had been drinking his coffee and nearly

choked when he heard the amount of the fine. "Ten percent?"

She grinned. "We have a long history of not getting along. During the 1920s there were several fights about water rights. Things got so bad that a couple of cowboys were killed. The Texas legislature enacted a law saying that if either a Fitzgerald or a Darby interfered with water rights again, both families would lose their ranches." She made an *X* over her heart. "I swear it's true. You can look it up."

"I believe you. I just didn't realize there was so much bad blood between the two families. How did it start?"

"About a hundred and forty years ago two friends came to Texas and settled in Lone Star Canyon. Joshua Fitzgerald and Michael Darby were young, fearless and interested in making their fortune. They had neighboring cattle ranches, sharing everything from winter feed to bulls."

Nora paused. She knew the history of the two families because she'd heard stories about them all her life. What would it have been like to live back then? she wondered.

"Joshua Fitzgerald decided it was time for him to settle down so he sent back east for a wife. A mail-order bride."

Stephen raised his eyebrows. "A woman, huh? I can see where this is going. I'll bet she made trouble."

Nora leaned forward. "Don't even think about going there, Dr. Remington. This feud wasn't started by the women of the family, but by the men."

Trixie arrived with their food and set the large plates in front of them. "You two seem to be getting along real nice,'' she said speculatively. ''Any chance you're reconsidering your opinion on men, Miss Nora?''

''Not really, Trixie, but thanks for asking.'' She smiled at the waitress, wished she were anywhere but here, then cut into her meat loaf. When she took a mouthful and started chewing, she noticed that Stephen was looking at her. Instantly, heat flared on her cheeks. No doubt he was learning a whole lot more about her than he'd wanted.

''You could eat,'' she said after she'd swallowed. She pointed at his plate. ''Your chicken is getting cold.''

He picked up his knife and fork. ''Please continue with your story. I'm all ears.''

Unfortunately he was more than that. He was good-looking, in a nerdy way, and kind. He didn't seem frightened of her, which was something she hadn't experienced in a while. Most men she knew thought of her as a fire-breathing, man-hating dragon.

''Joshua's mail-order bride wasn't impressed with her groom. Unfortunately Joshua fell for her hard and fast. He tried everything he could to win her heart, but after a year she left him. They were divorced shortly after that.''

''Let me guess,'' he said. ''She married Michael Darby.''

''About three days after her divorce was finalized. It seems that she and Michael had fallen in love at first sight and the feelings had never faded. Joshua didn't take kindly to being cuckolded by his best friend. From that time forward, the Darbys and the Fitzgeralds became bitter enemies.''

Stephen nodded when she was finished. ''I can see

how something like that would upset former friends, but not enough for a feud to last over a hundred years.''

"This is Texas," she reminded him. "We don't do things by halves out here."

"But you don't support the feud, do you?" He gave her an engaging smile. "After all, you're intelligent and very much a part of the present. I can't imagine someone like you caring about a silly family quarrel."

Nora had been busy thinking that Stephen wasn't such a bad guy after all and that maybe she'd misjudged him. But in one hot second, her opinion changed.

"It's very easy to judge a situation from the outside," she said calmly, which she didn't feel at all. "You've been here a few months. I've lived in Lone Star Canyon my entire life. I can trace my family tree for over six generations. We have traditions that mean something to us."

He finished chewing a bite of chicken and swallowed. "One of those traditions is the feud?" he asked.

"It's not that simple," she told him. She wasn't about to go into detail. There were personal reasons why she wasn't a huge fan of the Fitzgerald family.

"What about Katie?" he asked. "Do you hate her?"

Katie Fitzgerald was the oldest daughter and someone Nora had known since she started school. Katie was currently involved with Jack, Nora's oldest brother, and showing signs of being in love with him.

At one time Nora would have said yes, that she didn't like Katie very much, but now she wasn't so sure. For one thing, Katie had a son, Shane, who was the most amazing boy ever born. He and Nora had become friends. Some of Shane's charm and intelligence just might have come from his mother. For another thing, while they'd been growing up the Fitzgerald kids had seemed to have everything the Darby kids didn't. Reason enough for a young child to dislike someone. But things were different now. The Darbys finally had enough money. There weren't anymore worries about feeding and clothing seven kids. Besides, Nora had gotten to know Katie and had found out she wasn't such a horrible person. And she did seem to make Jack happy. Nevertheless she was a Fitzgerald. Which made the situation confusing.

"Let's talk about you for a change," Nora said, glaring at him. "Tell me the deep, dark secrets from your past."

He laughed. "You mean what's a good-looking, unmarried doctor like me doing in a place like this?"

"I'll accept the last part of the question."

"Fair enough." He set down his fork. "I was born and raised in New Jersey—the part that's not close to New York City. I wanted to be a doctor from the time I was little and I made it into medical school. I had a vision of being a simple country doctor. I wanted to take my patients from birth to death."

"Only if you're not planning on them living very long," she murmured.

"I'm talking," he complained. "You're supposed to listen attentively and then act suitably impressed. You're not supposed to interrupt."

For a second she thought he might be flirting with her, but that wasn't possible. Men didn't flirt with her—they ran in fear of their lives. "You don't know me very well if you expect that," she said.

"I know you well enough, Nora. I know you're compassionate, brave, determined and beautiful."

She blinked. He was kidding, right? Did he really think she was stupid enough to fall for a line like that?

"On what planet?" she asked, but her voice didn't sound as strong or contemptuous as she'd hoped, and instead of looking embarrassed, Stephen only looked knowing. As if he sensed her secrets and made allowances for them.

"As I was saying," he continued, "I wanted to be a country doctor. The old-fashioned kind of physician who takes care of every emergency, delivers babies and eases the suffering of the dying, along with everything in between. I got sidetracked with emergency room medicine for a few years, but now I'm here."

He finished the last of his chicken and wiped his mouth with a napkin. "Now you know my life history, why don't you tell me yours? For starters, why does everyone assume you're so unapproachable?"

Because she was, she thought, slightly confused by his curiosity. Most men found out about her reputation and went running in the opposite direction.

"I *am* unapproachable. I don't suffer fools gladly, I don't cater to male egos and I'm not interested in playing games."

Stephen looked at the woman sitting across from him. She'd gone from looking like a confident companion to glancing around like a trapped animal. She wasn't comfortable talking about herself and she wasn't comfortable with him. He half expected her to bolt from her seat and race to the door. Except he guessed that Nora would rather die than let him see that she was rattled by their dinner conversation.

He studied her smooth skin, the glossy dark hair spilling over her shoulders, the way her mouth gave away every emotion. Her mother was his patient and adored talking about her children, so he knew that Nora was twenty-eight. What had happened in her young life to make her so wary of men? And why did everyone in town know her secret but him?

Nora wasn't cold, he thought, remembering the waitress's comment that she could freeze a man to death. His nurse had implied that no one got to Nora. What he wanted to know was, why?

His interest surprised him. In the past two years he'd managed to avoid feeling anything for anyone except his patients. Emotionally he'd been numb inside. While he wasn't ready to care again—in fact he'd promised himself he would never fall in love with anyone else—he felt a stirring of interest that had little to do with the heart and much more to do with the mind…and the glands.

Nora engaged his brain and heated his blood. It was a tempting combination.

"You're not married," he said. It wasn't a question.

She set down her fork and pushed away her plate. "I don't actually think that's any of your business. Nor am I comfortable talking about my personal life with you."

"But you asked me all kinds of personal questions."

"I asked why you'd chosen to open your practice here."

He leaned forward and grinned. "Actually you

asked about deep, dark secrets in my past. Sounds pretty personal to me.''

"Fine. You chose to answer and I didn't."

She was prickly, all right, he thought. A challenge. Maybe he needed a good challenge in his life. Imagining Nora yielding to him, hissing even as she purred, stirred more than his blood.

"I'd like to see you again," he said. "How about dinner tomorrow night?"

She looked at him as if he'd suddenly sprouted purple horns and a tail. "You're insane. I don't *date*.'' The word was laced with both incredulity and contempt.

"Why not?"

It was a simple-enough question. She opened her mouth, closed it, then opened it again. Sound emerged, but it was more of a splutter than a reply. Finally she simply tossed her napkin on the table, slid out of the booth and hurried toward the door.

Stephen watched her go. He wasn't looking for the love of his life. He'd had that once and lost her. But he was willing to admit that he was lonely. Maybe it was time to change that. As the ever-prickly Miss Nora Darby didn't seem to be looking for anything permanent, either, maybe they could find a way to help each other.

Because he was willing to bet that if she didn't date much, she didn't get a chance to do other things. And just watching her move had told him she would probably do those other things very, very well.

Nora felt too crabby to sleep. She wanted to pretty up her emotions with words like *angry* or *keyed up*, but the truth was she was just plain crabby. Who was that man and what made him think that he had the right to…to…

She collapsed onto a sofa in her living room and sighed. Okay, all he'd done was ask her out. Was that so terrible? Didn't men ask women out all the time?

Maybe, she thought, trying to hang on to crabby in favor of feeling wistful. But men didn't ask her out. Not anymore. Not when she could verbally eviscerate them and frequently did. Not when she had a reputation of being difficult, stubborn and the kind of woman a man left at the altar.

She sighed and grabbed one of her floral-print pillows. She tucked the square against her chest and hugged it close. The worst of it was she'd been tempted to accept Stephen's invitation. For one brief second she'd thought about saying yes. Which was crazy.

Except… Nora shifted until she was curled up on the sofa. A part of her had sort of enjoyed her dinner with Stephen. He didn't seem intimidated by her. She didn't get out all that much anymore. Not just because she didn't date but because all her girlfriends had married and were starting families. They didn't have time for dinners out and she was usually too busy to break for lunch.

"I'll make new friends," she told herself softly. "Friends who are single like me." She vowed to start searching these mythical folks out the following day, despite the fact that most single females in Lone Star Canyon were either under twenty or over sixty-five.

"We'll do things together. I won't be reduced to accepting invitations from a man who spells his name with a 'ph' instead of a 'v,' like normal people. A man from Boston, or worse, New Jersey."

That decided, Nora thought about standing up and getting ready for bed. Between the tornado and her unexpected stint of nursing, she'd had a busy day. She was tired, she thought as her eyes drifted closed. But right now she felt too comfortable to move. Instead she would just...

The man's hands were warm and smooth and strong. Not sissy hands, but powerful and lean, with long fingers that knew exactly where to touch her. Despite being curled up on the sofa, Nora found herself arching toward those questing fingers that explored first her arm, then her shoulder. She trembled at the feel of his heat against her bare skin. She—

Bare skin? Nora opened her eyes and realized she was lying naked on her sofa. And she was no longer alone. Stephen Remington crouched next to her. Instead of his slacks, dress shirt and white coat, he wore jeans and a cable-knit sweater. Far too dressed, she thought hazily.

"Tell me about your past," he murmured, then kissed the sensitive skin just below her ear.

"Don't want to," she managed to say, between a gasp of erotic excitement and a soft cry of pleasure.

His strong hands urged her to shift onto her back. She did so, tossing the pillow away. He kissed her cheek, her chin, but when she tried to press her lips to his, he turned away. Before she could protest, he cupped her breasts. Thumb and forefinger teased her nipples, making her cry out and arch into his caress. She was on fire. She couldn't remember the last time a man had touched her, but it had been far too long. Celibacy was the downside of not getting involved, she thought, her mind thick with long-denied passion.

He continued to stroke her curves. He pressed

kisses to her belly, then moved lower. She shifted so that he could kiss her most intimate place of all. For a second there was nothing, then the perfect wonder of his tongue tasting her, teasing her, making her tilt her hips toward him and desperately call his name. Her body tensed and spiraled closer and closer to her point of release. She'd never been so ready so fast.

But before she could climax, he stopped. She opened her eyes and stared at him in disbelief. "What's wrong?" she asked.

"Nothing."

She reached to touch his head, his face, his hair. She was on fire and she would die if he didn't continue, didn't finish.

"Please," she breathed, holding him tightly. "Don't stop. Don't."

Nora woke with a start. She was still curled up on the sofa, clutching the pillow to her belly. Confusion filled her, then cleared as she realized it had been nothing more than a dream. A stupid dream that didn't mean anything.

She sat up and realized that while her mind might have figured out it was just a dream, her body was less aware of what was going on. She was aroused and ready to make love. To Stephen Remington of all people. How dare he get into her mind and mess with her that way? How dare he—

She moaned as she remembered the feel of his mouth against her body, then she shivered. She'd spent a couple of hours with the guy and he'd invaded her sleep? What was going on?

Nora vowed that whatever it was she would figure

out the problem, then fix it. She wasn't interested in having a man in her life. Not now, not ever. They were annoying and difficult and not for her. Not even Dr. Stephen Remington.

Chapter Three

"I didn't expect to see you here."

Nora froze at the sound of the too-familiar voice. The voice of the man who had haunted her sleep for the past two nights, invading her time of rest and assaulting her with hot kisses and erotic touches that left her aroused and frustrated when she awoke.

She ignored him by focusing on her client—an elderly lady stretched out on a chair, with her neck propped on the edge of the shampoo bowl in a back room of the Lone Star Retirement Village.

"Don't distract her," Mrs. Bailey said in her wavering voice. The white-haired, birdlike woman was nearly ninety. "Nora is busy making me beautiful. It takes longer these days than it used to."

"I would never dream of getting in the way of a lovely woman and her appointment with beauty," he said. "I just wanted to say hello to my favorite hair-dresser."

Nora was wrist-deep in shampoo and hair, but she couldn't help glancing at Stephen as he leaned against the door frame of the small room. He wore a white coat over a dust-colored shirt and brown slacks and there was a knowing look in his dark eyes. As if he suspected she'd spent the past couple of nights dreaming about him.

"Not likely," she muttered, referring more to him guessing her secret than to her being his favorite hair-dresser.

"It's true," he protested. "You're the only hair-dresser I know."

She nearly snorted at the adolescent comment. "Aren't you the clever one? How very humorous. It's amazing that I can keep upright, what with the laughter coursing through my body at that one. Gee, Doc, if medicine doesn't work out, you have a career in stand-up comedy at the ready."

He didn't budge. Worse, he didn't even blink at her tirade. "Does the word *overkill* mean anything to you, Nora?"

"No. Some things can't be dead enough."

She gave him an insincere smile, then flipped on the water. When the fine spray heated to the correct temperature, Nora rinsed off her hands, then carefully removed the shampoo from Mrs. Bailey's white curls.

"I'd like to talk with you before you leave," he said, raising his voice to be heard over the sound of running water.

She had a strong urge to tell him that she didn't care what he wanted, but she didn't want to sound like a petulant child. She shrugged her acceptance of his statement, then felt more than saw him leave the room.

"Why don't you like Dr. Stephen?" Mrs. Bailey asked as Nora wrapped a towel around her head and helped her into a sitting position. "He's very nice. Besides, he's really a dish." Mrs. Bailey blinked her pale blue eyes and smiled. "I suppose you young people would say he's hot."

Nora wrinkled her nose. "I'm not going to say anything at all about the good doctor's appearance. I'm sure he's everything he should be. But I'm not interested."

"Nora, you can't hide from men forever."

"Why not?" The plan had been working so far. If not for those darned erotic dreams.

"Because you're a beautiful young woman who should be married with a family."

The elderly woman's words caused a tiny ache to take up residence in Nora's heart. "I wouldn't mind the kids," she said honestly. "In fact I'd like them very much. It's the husband I object to."

"Men aren't so bad."

"Neither is an allergy to shellfish. That doesn't mean I want one."

Mrs. Bailey chuckled. "Nora Darby, you're a pistol, girl. But mark my words. One day you're going to meet a man who sweeps you off your feet. You're going to lose your heart to him and then where will you be?"

"Running for my life."

"No. You'll be very happy."

Stephen looked up at the light knock on the entrance to the makeshift office he used when he was called out to the Lone Star Retirement Village. Nora Darby glared at him, her beautiful brown eyes snapping with temper, her hackles already raised as she prepared for the slight she was so sure was coming.

Stephen bit back a grin. Nora was the sexiest woman he'd ever seen—at least in person. He remembered a couple of adolescent fantasies that had come close. Today she wore her dark, curly hair pulled on top of her head in a ponytail. Curls tumbled down to the nape of her neck, where they teased the faintly tanned skin there. The temperature had climbed into the mid-eighties—not unusual for spring in Texas, or so he'd been told. In honor of the heat—or maybe just to torment him—Nora had dressed in a cropped short-sleeved white shirt that had impossibly tempting, tiny buttons that started at the valley between her breasts and continued to the hem of the shirt, at her waist. Her low-slung denim skirt left about two inches of skin bare around her middle. Long, tanned legs disappeared into worn cowboy boots.

"What did you want?" she asked, folding her arms under her breasts. The movement pulled the shirt higher, exposing more of her tummy.

Nora Darby had a body built for sin, he thought, amazed that he could feel heat flaring through his body. He hadn't wanted a woman in so long, he'd assumed that part of him had died...or at least been frozen. Apparently he'd only needed the right kind of inspiration to wake things up.

"What's that expression?" he asked. "The one about a woman being a long, tall drink of water?"

She rolled her eyes. "Yeah, yeah, I'm tall. Five-nine. Is that what you wanted to talk about? And while we're on the subject, I don't appreciate being ordered into the inner sanctum. I don't work for you.''

''It wasn't an order,'' he said, motioning for her to take the chair on the opposite side of his desk. ''It was a request.''

She ignored his invitation and stayed by the door. ''You didn't say please.''

She was twenty kinds of trouble, he thought, holding in yet another grin. Damn, she made him feel alive and as randy as a sixteen-year-old spying on cheerleading practice.

''Please,'' he said, rising to his feet and walking around to stand behind the chair. ''I would be most honored if you would be so kind as to give me a few minutes of your time.''

Her eyebrows drew together in a scowl, but she tossed her head and made her way to the chair. When she plopped down, he returned to his own seat.

''I don't like you,'' she said before he could broach a different subject. ''You've got the entire town convinced you're a wonderful doctor, so kind, so handsome. I don't believe a word of it.''

She was defensive, he thought, feeling a surge of pleasure. Which meant she felt threatened. Did he get to her? Maybe his physical reaction to her wasn't completely one-sided.

''Thank you for your candor,'' he said, leaning forward and resting his hands on his desk. ''What I wanted to talk to you about was the women you see when you're here.''

He read her thoughts as clearly as if she'd printed them on paper. She wasn't sure why he was ignoring her comment about not liking him. She'd expected some kind of reaction—perhaps a defense of his practice. But Nora didn't threaten him. Quite the opposite. He didn't know why she wanted to play the prickly virgin, but he didn't object to her following a script, as long as she didn't expect the same from him.

"What about the women I see?" she asked, latching on to a new perceived slight. "You think it's silly or a waste of time. That they're old women and having their hair done or painting their nails doesn't matter." Fire flashed in her beautiful eyes. Her full mouth curled in disdain.

"I might not have your medical degree, Dr. Remington, but I know people. Especially women. I don't care if they're ten or a hundred, they care about their appearance. Feeling pretty reminds them they're alive, and in a good way that pain and illness can't. I come out here every week and see my regulars. They're important to me. In a way, that's part of the service I provide. It's not all about curlers and nail polish. Some of it is about connecting. Making them feel that someone knows who they are and cares about them."

As she spoke, her breathing increased, making her breasts rise and fall in a most provocative way. It was nearly enough to distract Stephen from her words. Nearly, but not quite.

"Stop assuming the worst, my little hellcat," he said calmly. "I'm not being critical or judging what you do. As a physician I know the value of treating a patient's soul as well as the body. I applaud your efforts. I encourage them. If a regular client of yours doesn't have the money for a shampoo and whatever it is you do, I would like you to tell me. I'm sure we can arrange something by way of a supplemental payment."

She blinked. "Oh."

"Yes, 'oh.' I also wanted to ask you to let me know if anyone you see seems depressed or lethargic. My patients matter to me and I want to be informed of any change in their condition. Especially those here at the retirement village."

Her lips pressed together as she absorbed his words. She cleared her throat. "I can do that."

He rose to his feet. "What? No witty comeback, no scathing comment?"

Her gaze didn't meet his. Instead she seemed to focus on the pocket of his lab coat. "Not at this time."

He had the strongest urge to walk around the table and kiss her. Just cup her cheek and lay one on her until they were both breathless. But he couldn't. Not yet.

"How disappointing," he said quietly, referring to the kiss that wouldn't be as much as the lack of snappy comeback. "Maybe next time."

She gaped at him like a fish. While she was still in shock, and relatively docile, he made his escape, chuckling all the way.

"Like I want to be here," Nora grumbled to herself a couple of days later as she pulled into the open area in front of the main house at the Darby ranch.

Her mother had issued a dinner invitation, and when Nora had tried to get out of it, Hattie had informed her it was a command performance. Death and dismemberment were the only excuses for lack of attendance. She glanced at her left hand and the broken ring-finger nail. She doubted that would count with her mother, so here she was.

She parked her car next to Katie's Explorer. Katie and her son, Shane, had been living on the ranch for more than a month now. Nora climbed out of her car and frowned. Katie had moved in temporarily, until her new house was built. Shouldn't it be finished by now? Maybe the two Fitzgeralds could leave the Darby ranch and go to their own home. Wouldn't that be nice? Or Katie could leave Shane behind. That would be even better.

Pleased at the thought, Nora hurried up the steps and entered the house. "Hi," she called as she stepped into the living room. "It's me."

She had planned to say more, to step forward to hug her mother and maybe tease her brother, but all thoughts fled her brain. One second she was in complete command of her senses and the next she was a blubbering idiot. All because Stephen Remington stood by the fireplace, a can of beer in his hand, looking for all the world as if he belonged there. No doubt he'd been invited by her mother in a futile attempt at matchmaking. She barely noticed anyone else in the room.

Her heart began to stutter and thump in her chest. Her legs grew weak and suddenly her entire body felt about twenty degrees hotter. Just setting eyes on Stephen was enough to remind her of the erotic dreams she'd been having. Dreams she couldn't seem to make stop. Night after night she found herself caught up in sensual wonder, with him touching her and her begging him to make love with her. Every morning she woke up aroused, unfulfilled and confused.

"Hello, Nora," her mother said warmly, rising to her feet and holding out her arms. "You look lovely as always."

Nora moved forward automatically. She hugged her mother, then helped her back into her seat. "How are you feeling?"

A few months before, Hattie had fallen while barrel racing at a friend's barbecue. She'd required surgery and physical therapy to heal her injuries. Nora and her brother Jack had been torn between admiration for their fifty-something mother's zest for life and frustration that she would take such risks. Still, Hattie had never been one to follow the rules.

"I'm wonderful," her mother said, smiling and patting the cushion next to her. "I'm down to weekly physical therapy, and I'll be riding by the end of the month."

"Riding? You can't be serious."

Nora nodded at her brother, who sat in the sofa opposite, then turned her attention to the woman sitting next to him. Katie Fitzgerald was blond, petite and pretty. As a teenager Nora had been taller than all the boys and had never felt as if she would fit in. Perfect Katie Fitzgerald had been the center of attention, smart *and* popular. Nora still felt like a gangly colt around the other woman.

"Is it all right for my mother to ride?" Nora asked.

Katie grinned. "You think she's going to listen to me? I'm just her physical therapist. Hattie is her own woman. You know that as well as anyone."

Nora sighed. Katie was right. She patted her mother's hand. "Just be careful."

"You could ask me to tell her it isn't wise," Stephen said from his place by the hearth. "After all, I'm her doctor."

Nora wanted to say, "Don't remind me," but that would sound too juvenile. "I guess I'm going to have to trust my mom to be more careful this time,'' she said, avoiding Stephen's gaze.

She hated that she was actually afraid to talk to the man. As if by engaging him in conversation she would inadvertently reveal what was in her mind. She glanced around the spacious living room and saw Shane, Katie's son, sitting in a chair by the window and playing a handheld video game.

She rose and crossed to him. As she approached, the blond-haired, blue-eyed boy looked up at her. His small glasses rested halfway down his nose. He pushed them back with an automatic gesture, then held out the game to her.

''Are we saving the universe?'' she asked as she took the game and plopped down on the floor next to him.

''Yup. But I've got a really high score.''

She raised her eyebrows. ''And you don't think I can beat you?''

Shane grinned. ''No way. You're a grown-up *and* a girl.''

''Be careful about the girl insults,'' Stephen warned. ''Nora doesn't take kindly to those.''

''Ignore him,'' Nora whispered, and pressed a couple of buttons on the keypad. ''Is this where I remind you I can get to a higher level than you on the space warrior game?''

''Just a couple of times,'' Shane told her.

''I see. And how many times have we played?''

Shane leaned forward and rested his bony elbow on her shoulder. She didn't mind the slight discomfort, or the weight of him as he leaned on her. ''Maybe three times.''

''And I beat you on how many of those games?''

"All three."

"Do you still want to talk about girls not having the skills?"

He giggled. "But that doesn't count."

"Oh, it doesn't, does it?" She tossed the game onto the cushion, then turned quickly and began tickling him. "I say it counts a lot, young man. I say it counts more than anything."

Shane fell back into the chair, laughing and shrieking, pushing her fingers away from his ribs, then protesting when she stopped. Finally, he slid off the chair and settled onto her lap. Nora might be ambivalent about her brother's relationship with Katie Fitzgerald, but she was a hundred percent sure about Katie's wonderful son. Nora adored Shane.

The remaining adults were discussing the rebuilding efforts after the tornado. Nora wrapped her arms around Shane and let her gaze drift around the room. She remembered a time when the furniture in the house had been shabby and Hattie had stretched every penny to the breaking point. In the past few years, that had changed. A combination of Jack's expert management of the ranch and an influx of cash from newly found oil on the property had given the Darby family a taste of prosperity.

Much of the old house had been renovated, including the wood floors in this room and the entire kitchen. Worn furniture had been replaced. Nora was pleased that there was finally money in the bank to see the ranch through future tough times. Jack and Hattie had also put money in trust for all seven of the Darby children. Nora was already eligible to start taking out her share, but she didn't know what she would spend it on. She'd decided to keep her nest egg in the bank where it could grow steadily.

Her brother gave Katie a knowing look, then stood and left the room. Nora watched him go. Something was up, she thought, wondering what secrets Katie and Jack might share.

Plenty, she realized a couple of minutes later when Jack returned carrying a chilled bottle of champagne along with a smaller bottle of sparkling apple cider. Hattie produced a tray of half a dozen champagne glasses.

"We have an announcement," Jack said, holding out his hand to Katie, then drawing her to her feet. He put his arm around her and gazed lovingly into her big blue eyes.

Shane turned to grin at Nora. He practically vibrated with happiness. "They're gettin' married," he said in a not-so-subtle whisper.

All the adults, except for Nora, laughed. It's not that she was unhappy…exactly…she just wasn't sure *what* she felt.

"That's right," Jack confirmed. "Katie has done me the honor of agreeing to be my wife. Shane will be my son."

The boy pushed off Nora and flew to Jack's side. Nora watched as her brother scooped Shane up in his arms and held him close. Hattie wrestled with the champagne bottle until Stephen rescued her and expertly popped the cork.

"The best part of this is I get a new house," Hattie said, holding out the tray so Stephen could fill everyone's glass. Katie served the sparkling cider to her son.

"They're going to live in this house," her mother

continued, "while I have a charming new place built for myself."

"Sounds like a great idea," Nora said, still not sure what she should make of the situation.

She stared at her brother and his fiancée who were gazing lovingly into each other's eyes. Married? To a Fitzgerald? Jack couldn't possibly. Nora sighed. Of course he could. She'd seen how the two of them looked at each other. Katie and Jack made each other very happy. They would be crazy to walk away from the opportunity.

Nora scrambled to her feet and took the champagne Hattie offered, then raised her glass as Stephen proposed a toast to the lucky couple. The sparkling liquid bubbled on her tongue, but she couldn't actually taste the sweetness.

"Are you all right with this?" Stephen asked as he moved next to her. "You look like you're in shock."

Normally she would have told him to mind his own business, or offered some other kind of witty comeback, but her mind was still absorbing the news.

"I'm fine," she said slowly. "I'm surprised, although I guess I shouldn't be. Katie's been staying on the ranch for several weeks now and it's been obvious that they care about each other."

"So you don't mind your brother getting married?"

She stared at the man in front of her. For once she was able to ignore the heat flaring through her body and the fact that she knew exactly how he would touch and kiss her if they ever made love.

"I'm not a shrew," she told him. "I want Jack to be happy. He deserves this. Katie is very nice. I know she's good for him, and Shane is a treasure."

"But she's a Fitzgerald."

"We can't all be perfect."

Stephen smiled then. A slow, male smile that made her aware that if he stepped just a little closer he could touch her bare arms and maybe even kiss her. Her breath caught as she imagined what it would be like to feel his skin on hers for real, and not just in her dreams.

Her mouth went dry at the thought. Her legs quivered slightly and there was a definite warmth flowing out from her belly.

"Nora?"

She turned at the sound of her name and saw Katie standing next to her. Petite, blond Katie wearing a pretty blue dress and looking like a perfect china doll. Nora sighed. She was tall. She would always be tall. Sometimes she even enjoyed being tall. If only there weren't so many short people around.

"I'm happy for you," Nora said quickly. "I mean that. I'm not a mean person, just crabby on occasion."

Katie gave her a grateful smile. "I know there have been some problems between our two families."

"Yeah. A hundred-plus years of feuding."

"I don't want it to be like that anymore." Katie's expression turned earnest. "I want us to be friends."

Nora swallowed and was a little surprised to find she wanted that, too. As if her family wasn't big enough already. "That sounds good," she murmured, then had to clear her throat.

"About the house. Jack and I were going to rebuild his place. I mean, I know I don't belong here. I'm selling the place I bought because Jack needs to live on the ranch." She cleared her throat. "The thing is

Hattie decided she wanted a new place for herself. She insisted Jack, Shane and I live here.'' Katie's hold on her glass tightened. ''I sort of got trapped into the situation.''

Nora touched the smaller woman's shoulder. ''Stop saying that. You're marrying the oldest Darby son. That makes this house your home. It's always been that way, Katie. You know that. As for Hattie, if my mom didn't really want a charming new house of her own, you couldn't pry her out of here with a crowbar. You know that, too.''

''You sure you don't mind?''

''As much as I would like the title, I'm not the queen of the world. I want you and Jack to be happy. I mean that.''

''Good.'' Katie smiled again. ''The wedding is going to be fairly soon. We don't want a long engagement. Also, we don't want a big fuss, so it's only going to be friends and family attending. My father didn't take the news very well, so I'm not sure if he'll be coming, but the rest of my family will be there.''

Katie didn't have to spell it out for her. Nora knew exactly what her future sister-in-law meant. David Fitzgerald, Katie's oldest brother, would be at the wedding.

''I'm a big girl,'' Nora said with a lightness she didn't feel. ''I can handle David.''

Before Katie could respond, Jack called her over to his side. Nora watched the couple step close to each other, as if they'd always been together. She sighed. ''I think they'll be very happy.''

''I think you're right.''

Stephen's voice surprised her. She'd forgotten he

was standing next to her. Now he took a step closer, which meant that she could almost feel his heat.

"You did a nice thing," he said softly. "Katie was afraid that you'd be upset about the engagement and the fact that Hattie wants them to have the house."

Nora grimaced but didn't say anything. In her capacity as a physical therapist, Katie spent a lot of time consulting with Stephen. Of course they would talk.

"Katie makes my brother happy. That's all I've ever wanted."

"And you're really fine with this?"

"I already told you. I think it's wonderful. Jack will be a great husband to Katie and an even better father to Shane."

Stephen did the unthinkable. He actually put his arm around her. Nora was so stunned she nearly dropped her drink.

"Now that we've cleared that up," he said conversationally, as if he touched her like this all the time. "Answer me another question. Who's David?"

Chapter Four

Stephen tried not to read too much into the situation, but Nora actually trembled in his embrace. He could feel the slight shiver rippling through her as he kept his arm around her. The thought that he might make her nervous pleased him. She might be mouthy and ten kinds of prickly, but she wasn't immune. He found he didn't want her to be able to walk away and not think about him. Not when he spent so much of his time thinking about her.

After two years of not noticing another woman, he found himself fully aware of the one next to him. The light scent of Nora's perfume made him want to lean close and inhale the fragrance more fully. She wore a pale yellow sundress that left her arms bare. He had the strong urge to find the zipper tab and slowly lower it until the sleeveless, low-cut garment fell open. He was stirring to life and even enjoying the process.

From what he could tell, his reaction was specific to Nora. He wasn't intrigued by any other woman he'd met.

She gave him a quick, awkward smile, then side-stepped his embrace. In her high-heeled sandals, they were nearly the same height. She wore her beautiful dark hair pulled back in a braid. Her eyes were wide and mysterious, her mouth slightly parted and tempting.

"What do you want to know about David?" she asked, her voice almost a squeak.

She glanced around the living room as if concerned who might be listening to their conversation. But Jack and Shane were talking to each other while Hattie and Katie pored over a bride magazine.

David? Who was David? he wondered. It took him a minute to get up to speed. Then he remembered he'd asked her a question. Funny how being close to her and touching her, however casually, was enough to fry his brain.

"Katie said there would be family and close friends at the wedding," he said softly. "The implication was that could be a problem. You said you could handle David. So who is David?"

"Oh." She folded her arms across her chest, which pushed her breasts up and together, giving him an eyeful of impressive cleavage. She didn't just rank a Slippery When Wet warning sign; Nora was one of those woman who needed a Dangerous Curves Ahead marker.

She sighed. "I might as well tell you because if I don't, you'll hear it from someone else. And they'll get the story wrong."

"Why would I hear anything about him?"

She looked at him as if he wasn't very bright. "Because my brother is marrying a Fitzgerald. That will start all kinds of speculation. People will want to recap history."

"Good point. So what's the story?"

"David Fitzgerald is Katie's oldest brother," she said, sinking onto the sofa. He settled next to her, not as close as he would like, but still near enough to enjoy the scent of her perfume without being in slapping range. "We started dating in high school."

The information took a couple of seconds to sink in. "You dated a Fitzgerald?"

The question came out louder than he'd intended. Everyone in the room turned to look at him. Nora flushed, then sprang to her feet. "We'll go set the table," she told her mother. "Are we eating in the dining room?"

"Yes, dear." Hattie's gaze shifted from Stephen to her daughter and back. "That would be nice. Use the good china."

Nora stalked off. Stephen trailed after her. When they reached the dining room, she turned on him. "Don't do that," she instructed. "I don't need the pleasure of being humiliated in front of my family."

He held up both hands in a gesture of surrender. "Sorry. It slipped out. I just couldn't believe you'd dated a Fitzgerald. You're the rabid one about the feud. I would have thought you'd rather interspecies date than do that."

Color still stained her cheeks. Her mouth worked furiously, but no sound emerged. Finally she planted her hands on her hips. "Interspecies date?"

He tried not to smile. "I was making a point, Nora. I didn't actually mean it."

"You think I'm such a mutant that no man would want me? That I would be reduced to the local garter snake, or perhaps a zebra?"

"I hadn't actually thought of a garter snake." He reached forward and took her right hand in his. "I'm sorry," he repeated. "I wasn't trying to make fun of you or embarrass you in front of your family. You have to admit, given what I know about you and your views, the thought of you dating Katie's brother would be a little shocking."

As he spoke, he moved his thumb against the back of her hand. Her skin was smooth and soft and warm. He thought he detected a slight quiver, but he wasn't sure. Still, he must have done something right, because the light of battle drifted out of her eyes and some of her tension eased.

"I guess I can understand that," she admitted.

"So tell me what happened."

She pulled her hand free, then turned her back on him. "Have a seat," she said. "I'll set the table."

"I'll help," he offered.

She gave him a withering glance. "You'd just get in the way. You can sit down and listen or you can leave."

"Have you always been this bossy?" he grumbled, even as he took a seat on one of the spare chairs against the wall.

"Always," she told him.

She disappeared into the kitchen, then reappeared seconds later carrying a cloth. She started at one end, carefully wiping down the large, rectangular table.

The dining room was good-sized, about twenty-by-fifteen with a chair rail that went all the way around the room. The table had six chairs around the perimeter, but there were another six lined up along the wall. To the east was a tall hutch and opposite that was a buffet table.

"As I was saying before you started screaming loud enough to wake the dead," she said, not looking at him as she spoke, "David and I dated all through high school. Both of our families were shocked, although my mom was more okay with it than his dad. Everyone thought it would end when David went off to college, but it didn't. We got engaged the summer I turned twenty. It was supposed to be a long engagement—at least until David graduated. I guess everyone thought the romance would fizzle out."

She moved as she talked, taking a tablecloth from a deep drawer in the buffet and smoothing it over the table. Then she collected napkins and silverware. She worked with the easy grace women have when they perform the familiar. Her body swayed, her hips shifted in an entrancing rhythm.

"Did the romance fizzle out?" he asked in an effort to distract himself.

"Not for me. I can't speak for David, although I guess his actions told the truth loud enough." She straightened and faced him. "After David graduated, we set a date for the following spring. I had long finished beauty school and was working at the Snip 'n Clip. Aaron, David's father, came to see me one evening when I was closing the shop."

She paused, then shuddered, as if after all this time, Aaron's words still had the power to wound. "He looks so much like David, just an older version. But he's nothing like his son. David was always funny, gentle and kind. Aaron stared at me like he wanted to rip me apart using his bare hands." She clutched the back of the chair in front of her. "He said that no son of his was going to marry a Darby. That he would disown David if he tried and that his son wasn't strong enough to walk away from the family fortune."

Stephen wanted to ask her if she was kidding. This was the twenty-first century, not feudal England. "What happened?"

She shrugged. "I told David and he promised everything would be fine. That he would love me forever. Then he went away."

She walked to the hutch and removed six dinner plates. "I guess Aaron sent him. That part was never clear. One minute he was in Lone Star Canyon and the next, he was gone. At first he wrote me every day. He said not to worry. That he was working on a ranch that belonged to a friend of his father's. He was learning a lot and missed me. He swore he would return in time for the wedding. Then the letters became less and less frequent."

She set the plates in place, then brought out glasses. She gave Stephen a smile that trembled a little at the corners. "He returned two weeks before the wedding, but he didn't come home alone. Instead he brought his new bride of less than a month, who was already nearly two months pregnant." She put the glasses at each place setting. "You'll meet Fern and their daughters at Jack and Katie's wedding."

Stephen didn't know what to say. He'd expected something bad, but he hadn't considered that Nora would have been so betrayed. He frowned as he remembered hearing something about her father running out on his family when she was eleven or so. Obviously she had a history of men letting her down.

No wonder she wasn't thrilled with the males of the species. Knowing about her past made her prickly personality easier to understand.

"I don't care that they're going to be at the wedding," she continued. "I'm long over him. However, I do have my pride. We live in a small town and people talk."

She didn't want pity. He knew that instinctively. Nora would hate any whispers from those who felt sorry for her. He found himself feeling oddly protective of her, which was crazy. Nora would have him for lunch on a platter if she knew what he was thinking. But he couldn't help wondering how different she would be if only there had been a trustworthy man in her life. Someone who had kept his promise to love her forever.

Not that it could be him, he reminded himself. He wasn't into love and forever. Not anymore. Friendship was allowed. Maybe even being lovers, but nothing more.

"Everyone I've met has great respect for you," he said at last. "If they pity anyone I suspect it's David."

She smiled for real then, her eyes dancing with humor. "Have you met Fern?"

"No."

"It's the only good part of the story. It turns out she hates the ranch and everything to do with it.

Later that evening Stephen followed Nora into the kitchen to collect dessert. Dinner had gone well, he thought. Everyone had treated him like a member of the family. Even Nora had been almost nice.

She was still a prickly pear of a woman. While he

didn't mind that part of her, knowing the reason made it even easier to understand and accept.

She moved around the kitchen with the ease of someone who was familiar with where everything went. He had to remind himself that Nora had grown up on this ranch...in this house. He thought of her as being a part of Lone Star Canyon, but not as someone who had lived on a ranch. He couldn't see her riding the herd, or whatever it was ranchers did. She was too beautiful, too sexy.

"So do you know how to ride a horse?" he said.

She turned to look at him, her expression confused. "Where did that question come from?"

"I was just wondering."

"Of course I can ride. I grew up here. I can rope, bring in the herd, inoculate the calves, whatever needs doing. I'd rather not." She held out one perfectly groomed hand and wiggled her fingers. Light reflected off the shimmering polish she wore. "Ranch work is death on my manicure."

He leaned against the center island while she flipped on the coffeemaker. "You aren't the only one who left the ranching world," he said. "I heard you and Katie talking about Katie's sister Josie. She's the one who moved to California, isn't she?"

Nora had collected a half dozen dessert forks. She set them on the counter and sighed. A sad smile tugged at the corners of her mouth.

"Josie Fitzgerald and I used to be best friends back before we knew we were supposed to hate each other. We were the same age and in the same grade. We were both tall and too skinny and we ganged up together to beat up any boys who teased us."

He could picture a younger Nora, in pigtails, with

grass stains on her shorts and T-shirt and nearly permanently scraped knees. He found himself wishing he'd known her back then.

"So she's the only Fitzgerald you talk to these days? Except for Katie, of course."

Nora shook her head slowly. "No. We lost touch. Isn't that crazy?"

She didn't seem to expect an answer so he didn't say anything.

She raised her head and looked at him. "Josie went to college in California and I went to beauty school. We sort of drifted apart. She invited me to her wedding, but I didn't go. Now I don't remember why. Maybe I didn't want to see David, I don't know." She frowned. "I heard she became a teacher. Her marriage ended. So much life between us and I wasn't a part of any of it. Yet there had been a time when we were practically joined at the hip."

A bit of information teased at his memory. "Wasn't Josie the one who was just in a bad car accident?"

Nora nodded. "About a month ago. Katie was telling me about her latest surgery. Apparently Josie's entire face is being rebuilt, along with one of her legs. She's going to have surgeries on and off for the next year."

Stephen knew he was treading on dangerous territory, but he couldn't help himself. He stepped close enough to touch Nora and place his hand on her bare arm. "You might want to get in touch with her," he said gently. "Life in a hospital room can be very grim and lonely. I'm sure she'd appreciate hearing from you, regardless of how much time it's been."

He expected her to bite his head off, or at the very

least, attempt to reduce him to a quivering puddle. Instead she nodded in agreement. "You're right. I will do that. I want to—"

Her entire body stiffened. She was no longer looking at him and he turned to see what had captured her attention. Sitting in the center of the island was a tall cake box. From this side, he could see through a small plastic window. The dessert Hattie had chosen for their meal was a two-layer replica of a wedding cake.

Nora moved away from him and carefully opened the box. When the white cardboard sides were flat, she gently touched a tiny sugary, pink flower. "This was my mother's idea," she told him. "Hattie was born a romantic."

He wanted to ask if Nora was, too. Had she had hopes and dreams at one time in her life, only to have them stolen from her by the men who claimed to love her and then left?

The idea of a wounded, potentially emotionally lonely woman should have sent him screaming into the night. Instead he found himself wanting to move closer to her. He was lonely, too. Maybe they could offer each other comfort. But how did a man go about wooing a woman like her and live to tell the tale?

Nora waited at the signal, her gaze drawn back to her rearview mirror. The pair of headlights was still there. The same headlights that had followed her from the ranch. Damn the man. What did he think he was doing?

When the light turned green, she stepped on the gas and sped down the street. She slowed to turn into her neighborhood, making first a right, then a left and another right. She slipped into her driveway with the ease of long practice, then turned off the engine. Before she could even get her key out of the ignition, a car pulled in behind her.

That was it, she thought, fuming. She'd had enough. She jerked her keys free, grabbed them and her purse, then shoved open the door and climbed out onto her driveway.

It was a perfect Texas night. Cool, clear, with a million stars twinkling overhead. Nora was almost distracted by the beauty of the moment, but then she saw Stephen getting out of his car and her bad temper returned.

"What do you think you're doing?" she demanded when they were less than two feet apart. She was careful to keep her voice low. After all, it was ten on a weeknight and many of her neighbors had small children who would already be in bed.

Stephen didn't look the least bit ruffled by her display of temper. Come to think of it, he rarely seemed to notice when she exploded at him. If anything, her short fuse seemed to amuse him.

"I do not appreciate being followed," she continued when he didn't speak. "There are laws against stalking people. I don't care how you get your jollies, but do them somewhere else."

He folded his arms over his chest and raised his eyebrows. "Is that the best you can do?" he asked lazily. "I thought you'd be in a bigger snit."

"Snit? This is no snit. You may choose not to take me seriously, but you are making a mistake if you don't."

"Take you seriously or choose not to?" he asked with a low chuckle.

Her temper flared, and with it the need to stomp

her foot and scream in frustration. Instead she clenched her hands more tightly around her purse and glared at him. "If that's all you have to say, I'm going inside."

She spun on her heel and took a single step away from him.

"I wasn't following you," he said quickly. "I wanted to make sure you got home all right. It's late, you're driving alone. That was it. No ulterior motive."

She spun back to face him. "I'm twenty-eight years old. I've been driving for about twelve years. Amazingly enough I've managed to make it to the ranch and back multiple times without anyone checking on me. I'm going to go out on a limb and guess I'll be able to do it in the future. Thanks for worrying, but really, you can let this one go. There was the one kidnapping attempt, but I managed to elude my abductors, so relax."

She gave him an insincere smile. "Not to make you panic or anything, but I'm thinking of going to the grocery store tomorrow, all on my own." She loosened her grip on her purse and pressed one hand on her chest. "Oh, my. Do you think I'll survive?"

He leaned against his car. There was just enough street light for her to see the flash of amusement in his hazel eyes. He thought this was funny? She blinked in confusion. Shouldn't he be running for cover about now?

"I'll bet there are a lot of guys who buy into your act," he said conversationally. "Men who think you're all mouth and not worth the trouble. So they back off. I'm guessing that's what you want, or you wouldn't bother with the ice princess act."

It was as if he'd read her mind, she thought in shock. Color flared on her cheeks. She could only hope that the darkness hid the blush from him. "It's not an act," she mumbled, taking a step back.

"Sure it is." He moved one step closer. "What I can't figure out is why. You're funny, you're sexy as hell, you're too smart for your own good. So why are you so determined to keep men running for cover?"

His compliments, however backhanded, made her blush deepen. Did he mean them? Did he really think she was sexy? "Maybe I don't share your high opinion of your gender. I'd rather be alone."

"Would you? I'm not sure I believe that."

"Of course you don't. My wanting to be alone doesn't cater to your ego."

He took another step nearer. He was standing way too close, she thought as her chest tightened and her throat went dry. But she wasn't going to be the one to move away. Never show weakness. It was one of her best rules.

"You know what my ego says?" he asked.

She rolled her eyes. "That you're a brilliant doctor, incredibly good-looking and any woman would be lucky to have you."

"Thank you," he said sincerely. "But we weren't talking about me."

This time she did stomp her foot in frustration. "I wasn't saying that about you. I don't think you're any of those things. I was telling you what your ego thinks of you. There's a difference."

He lowered his hands to his sides and stared deeply into her eyes. "Actually there isn't. You *do* think I'm all those things and it's killing you."

Her temper flared. "I never—"

But she didn't get to say what she "never" did because without warning he wrapped his arms around her, drew her close and kissed her.

Chapter Five

The real-life kiss was better than the ones in her dreams, which Nora hadn't thought possible. Worse, they'd barely started and she was already a quivering, willing puddle of desire. She tried to find it in herself to be angry, to be *anything* but needy, but she couldn't. Not when he was touching her and pressing his mouth to hers.

His arms felt strong as he held her close. His lips were firm yet yielding, warm, possessive and so incredibly tempting. Against her will, her body leaned into his and her hands somehow found their way to his shoulders, where they clung as if he were the only solid matter in an otherwise spinning world. All this after one chaste kiss. What would happen to her if he really started trying?

Then she realized she didn't care. Not right now.

The battle of the sexes was one she took seriously, but it was time for a temporary truce.

Stephen angled his head slightly, as if preparing to deepen the kiss. He moved against her mouth, touching every millimeter of her sensitized skin. Tingling started there and moved lower, making her breasts ache and that feminine part of her weep with almost forgotten need. She couldn't remember the last time she'd been held so perfectly and made to feel almost fragile. It didn't matter that in her high-heeled sandals she was almost his height and that she would never be anyone's idea of delicate. Something about the way he touched her and kissed her made her feel almost girlish.

She could feel his individual fingers as they splayed across her back. He shifted slightly, moving closer, then brushed his tongue against her lower lip. The perfect sensation made her blood rush through her at the speed of sound, heating every inch of her body, making her part her lips in welcome. He brushed her tongue with his, letting her taste his sweetness. As he entered her mouth, a keen vibration took up residence low in her belly. He was as perfect as he'd been in her dreams…maybe more perfect. Her sternness, her resolve to stay unmoved by any man, her very separateness disappeared as if it had never been. She wanted him with a desperation that terrified her. But instead of pulling away, she clung to him, running her fingers through his thick hair and flattening her breasts against his chest.

Need pulled at her, making her want to tear off his clothes. She wanted him naked, on top of her, taking her in a moment of passion so explosive they risked their very lives by participating. She wanted him to know that she already ached and hungered. She wanted to mingle the very essence of their beings until they ceased to be individuals and were only the miraculous joining of two perfectly matched spirits.

The intensity of her response horrified her. She didn't need any man—not even in bed. She was always in control. But the words had an empty sound and she found it difficult to concentrate on anything but the gentle stroking of his tongue and the feel of his hands sliding up and down her back. She arched into his touch like a cat begging to be stroked. When his hand moved lower, cupping her rear, her hips automatically shifted, pressing against his lower body. She felt the hardness of his arousal. A quick, heady thrill shot through her.

He pulled back slightly so he could tenderly kiss her face. First her cheeks, then her nose, her forehead and finally her chin. He nibbled on her ear, then trailed down her neck, making her shake and gasp and wonder if they could do it right there on the hood of her car.

The image of herself surrendering with such abandon nearly had her reaching for the buttons of his shirt. Then, somewhere nearby, she heard a door slam. Reality intruded with the subtlety of a dinosaur crashing a tea party. She stiffened, then straightened and pulled back. They were in her driveway! What was she thinking?

She hadn't been thinking, she realized as she tried to catch her breath. Her chest felt tight, as if her lungs could never fill up with enough air. The night was cool, but her skin was burning hot and her insides felt like melted butter.

Stephen shifted so that he was braced against her

car, then put his hands on her hips and drew her to him. But she'd already learned her lesson about getting too close to him. She jerked free of his touch.

"What do you think you're doing?" she demanded, hating the breathy quality of her voice. She'd wanted to sound powerfully outraged.

"Isn't it obvious? I'm going to kiss you again." He gave her a sexy smile. "We both liked it, so why not?"

Sensible question, she thought grudgingly. However, she didn't feel the least bit sensible.

"I can think of a dozen reasons not to do that again. This is crazy."

"Is it?" In the darkness of the night, his hazel eyes looked fathomless. "Why?"

She sputtered but couldn't come up with an answer.

He reached for her again, this time snagging her wrist. He tugged until she found herself standing between his splayed legs, although she was careful to keep their lower bodies from touching. If she felt his arousal again, she would lose all control and simply beg him to take her.

"The way I see it, it's fairly simple," he told her. "You're single and I'm single. From all that I've heard, the last thing you're looking for is a serious relationship. I have different reasons for my motivation, but the point is, I don't want to get involved, either."

His words should have eased her concerns but oddly, they made her feel sad. "What's your problem with getting involved?" she asked.

"That's not important. My point is we're both responsible adults who know how the game is played.

Why not take advantage of that? We could be friends.''

As he spoke his fingers had woven themselves between hers. He was stroking the back of her wrist—a neat trick that made her heart thunder and her breasts ache even more.

She deliberately pulled free of his touch and narrowed her gaze. ''My mother didn't raise a fool. You don't want to be friends, you want sex.''

He leaned so close, she thought he was going to kiss her again. But he didn't.

''So do you.''

He'd whispered the words, but they echoed in her brain like a shout. Damn him for telling the truth, she thought grimly. Between her long period of celibacy and the dreams she'd been having about him, she had all the resistance of melted snow.

''I resent the implication that I'm easy,'' she said stiffly.

Stephen laughed. ''Nora, you're many things, but easy isn't one of them. Trust me on this. You're about the most complicated woman I've ever known. But I'm not like those other men you know. I'm not frightened of you and you can't scare me away with your sharp tongue and quick wit. I think we could be good for each other. Both in and out of bed. We would go into the situation with everything clearly defined. I'm not looking for a string of bedmates. I want a lover—someone I can depend on and who will depend on me. Are you interested?''

She swallowed. He'd certainly spelled it all out, she thought, slightly stunned by his pronouncement. Lovers? As in monogamous bedmates? Sex and friendship without the worry of love and marriage? She didn't approve of marriage. It rarely worked out well for the woman.

"We need each other," he murmured, brushing his mouth against hers.

"I don't need anyone."

"Liar. You need me, big time. You're tired of being alone. We'd be great together and you know it."

As if to prove his point, he deepened the kiss, slipping between her parted lips and making her burn. She found herself wrapping her arms around him and leaning against his hard strength. She was so aroused that if he'd touched her intimately in any way, she would have lost control.

"I don't know that I even like you," she said when she finally found the strength to pull back.

He grinned. "Of course you like me. As you said, I'm brilliant and good-looking. What's not to like?"

"You have an ego the size of Texas," she muttered.

"You're just the woman to cut me down to size."

He gave her one last, hard kiss, then set her away from him. "Think about it," he told her as he headed for his car. "I'll be in touch."

She wanted to think of something perfectly brilliant and pithy to hurl after him, but her mind was completely blank. If she wasn't mistaken, this was the second time Stephen Remington had left her speechless.

"I really hate that," she said to herself as he waved and drove off. "I'm not going to think about him or his ridiculous proposition. Not for even one second," she promised herself. "I'm not interested and I would never agree. It's crazy, just like the man himself."

His soft response came to her as clearly as if he'd been there speaking directly into her ear.

"Liar."

Stephen slapped down the medical journal he'd been trying to read and glared at the phone. He hadn't seen Nora in a week. He'd left three messages for her—two at her house and one at her salon. She'd ignored them all. He'd expected her to play games; he just hadn't thought they would go on this long.

He rose to his feet and paced to the window. His office overlooked a side yard. The grass was slowly coming back to life and turning green while the flowering bushes were in full bloom. Spring had arrived in Lone Star Canyon. But while the rest of the world was enjoying the longer days and warm temperatures, he was stuck reliving a kiss he should have been able to forget fifteen minutes after it happened. Worse, Nora was giving him the brush-off.

How could she do that? The passion hadn't been all one-sided. He'd felt her arousal and her response to his kisses. She'd been trembling, overheated and willing. He knew that if they'd been somewhere slightly more private than her driveway, they probably would have made love that night.

He paused in his mental monologue and probed his heart. Did he mind that he was attracted to another woman? Did it break the rules?

He considered the questions and decided that as long as he didn't fall in love with anyone, he was allowed to experience all the wonders the human body had to offer. After over two years of feeling like one of the living dead, he was alive again. Unfortunately the woman responsible for his resurrection had disappeared from his life.

In addition to leaving messages, he'd been lingering after hours, hoping to catch a glimpse of her when she left her shop. He'd been hovering by the entrance to the medical office, checking out patrons at the local restaurants and generally acting like an adolescent with his first crush. Dammit, he was a grown man interested in having a very adult affair. If Nora couldn't handle that, she should simply tell him no.

He paced to his desk and perched on a corner. He understood her need for caution. After all, her past had left her bruised and not very trusting. But wasn't a week long enough to figure out if she was over that or not?

He folded his arms over his chest and raised his chin. Nora could keep playing this game if she wanted, he decided, but he was finished. As soon as Nurse Rosie left for the day, he was going to walk over to the Snip 'n Clip and confront Nora face-to-face. There wouldn't be any more games—just reasonable decisions about what was going to happen next.

That decided, he felt himself relax. He returned to his chair and picked up his medical journal. But before he could find his place and begin reading, there was a knock on his door.

"Come in," he called.

Nurse Rosie opened the door. "You have a visitor," she said. "Is this a good time for you to see her?"

His heart rate increased dramatically. Nora? Nurse Rosie's expression was completely neutral. "Show her in."

But the woman who entered his office wasn't Nora. Instead she was a petite redhead wearing black jeans and a gray short-sleeved sweater. She gave him a worried smile, then took the chair on the opposite side of the desk. Stephen thought she looked familiar but he couldn't place her.

"I'm Dr. Remington. How may I help you?"

"I'm Jill," she said. "I work across the street at the Snip 'n Clip."

Stephen nodded. That's where he'd seen the woman before. She'd been in the underground shelter the day of the tornado. "Is there a problem?"

"Sort of." Jill shrugged. "She's gonna kill me. I just know it. But it's been nearly a week and we're all really worried. Maybe you could go look at her and let us know if she's okay."

"Who is 'she' and what's wrong with her?"

"Oh. Sorry." Jill leaned toward him. "It's Nora. She's had a stomach bug for nearly a week. She can't keep any food down. She's weak and has a fever, but she's too stubborn to go to her doctor. Actually I think she's too sick to drive that far." She gave him a sheepish smile. "She, ah, drives across the valley to see a different doctor."

"Yes, I know," he said wryly. He was sure Nora would rather eat glass than claim him as her physician. Then he dismissed all personal thoughts and concentrated on the facts. "How high is the fever?"

"I'm not sure. Just over a hundred, I think."

He asked several more questions and copied down the answers. "I'll go see her right away," he promised the woman. "I suspect it's not that serious, but it sounds like, at the very least, she's dehydrated."

"Could you phone the shop afterward and let us

know that she's okay?'' Jill asked. She rose to her feet and pulled a business card out of her jeans pocket. ''I'm working until eight tonight, so whenever it's convenient.''

''No problem.''

Stephen was surprised to find himself feeling edgy as he collected supplies and explained the situation to Nurse Rosie. It was more than the concern he always felt for his ill patients, but he didn't stop to examine the emotions or figure out what they meant.

''Go away,'' Nora said from behind her still-closed door. ''I don't want to see you.''

Stephen stifled the urge to swear at her. Why was he surprised that she was being difficult? ''You're sick, I'm a doctor. It's a natural match. Now, let me in. Your friends are worried about you. Based on the symptoms they've described to me, you've had a stomach virus, but I want to rule out anything more dangerous. I'm guessing you haven't been eating or drinking, so you're dehydrated. That's why you feel so lousy and light-headed. I'm coming in, Nora. You can make it easy on both of us, or you can make it difficult, but the end result is going to be the same.''

There was a long moment of silence. ''Don't you sound all macho,'' she finally grumbled. He heard the sound of a lock being unlatched.

''I look terrible,'' she warned. ''Try not to visibly blanch.'' She opened the door and glared at him. ''I mean it.''

He took in her too-pale face and the dark circles under her eyes. Her normally full, curly hair had been pulled back into a thick braid. She wore a T-shirt and sweats, and her feet were bare.

He gave her a quick once-over and shrugged. "Okay, I didn't turn to stone. Now, let me in."

She mumbled something under her breath, but backed up to give him room to enter the house. He had a brief impression of color and comfortable furniture before she turned and started down the hall. As she walked, she braced one hand against the wall.

"I know it's not done in the best circles," she said, "but I can't stay standing very long. I'll have to entertain you in my bedroom." She paused but didn't turn around. "I really hate how that sounded. Don't you dare take it wrong. I'm too sick to personally do you any damage, but I have brothers very happy to defend my honor."

"I wasn't going to say a word."

He followed her into a spacious bedroom brightened by the light pouring in from several windows. He saw lace and too many throw pillows. Nora crawled back into the queen-size bed and pulled the covers up to her chest. Immediately her eyes drifted closed.

"Go away," she said. "I prefer to die alone."

"You're not going to die," he told her, pulling up the padded chair in the corner and setting his bag on the floor. "I'm here to prevent that." He pulled out a stethoscope and a thermometer. "When did the symptoms first start?"

She opened one eye. "You're not my doctor. You can't examine me."

"Actually I can. I have a degree and everything. That's why people call me *Doctor* Remington. Pretty cool, huh?"

Both eyes opened as she glared at him. "Number one—I don't think you're funny. Number two—we kissed. Therefore there's an ethical issue, isn't there? Besides, I have a perfectly good doctor, who is a woman, I might add. I'd rather see her.''

"You can't make the drive and she's unlikely to drive sixty miles for a house call. I'm here, I'm qualified, and as far as the kiss is concerned, while I'm acting as your physician, it never happened. I swear, I'll think only professional doctor thoughts.''

She eyed him warily. Her lips were pale and dry and her skin lacked its usual glow. His humor faded. "Nora, I think the worst of this is over, virus-wise, but I can't be sure unless I examine you. You're obviously dehydrated. I want to put you on an IV for a day or so to hydrate you, but I have to rule out other causes first. Now, quit acting like a brat and let me do my job.''

Her eyes closed. "And if I tell you that I don't like you very much?''

"I'd file the information away for later. It's not relevant to our current discussion.''

She sighed heavily. "Okay. Examine away.''

Twenty minutes later he settled back on his chair and looked at her. "Your fever is almost gone,'' he said, reviewing the chart he'd started. "Based on your symptoms, the length of your illness and your recovery, it's what I thought. A particularly nasty stomach virus. What you have to do now is give yourself a few days to heal. Unfortunately, you're dangerously dehydrated. My first thought is to put you in the hospital for a couple of days.''

He'd been expecting a reaction to his statement and Nora didn't disappoint him.

"What? Are you crazy? The hospital? Now? Where were you with your brilliant suggestions when

I was barfing my guts out? Isn't this a little like closing the barn door after the horse is gone? What good will that do?''

''I want to put in an IV to hydrate you and I don't want you alone until it comes out. Can you have someone stay with you for the next twenty-four to thirty-six hours?''

''Sure. My mom will drive into town just as soon as I call her.''

''Then I guess you can stay here.''

He set up the portable IV pole he'd brought with him and started her on the saline drip. He made a quick list of supplies, then called Hattie Darby and explained the situation. Nora's mother promised to leave the ranch within the half hour. She would stop at the store for the needed items and then make her way to Nora's. Stephen told her there was no rush. He was done for the day and would be happy to wait with Nora until Hattie arrived.

When he hung up the phone, Nora turned away, as if she hadn't been listening to everything he said.

''You'll start to feel better in a few hours,'' he said. ''Once you start hydrating, your energy level will increase.'' He paused to look at her. ''You had to know you were pretty sick. Why didn't you call or come by the office?''

She shifted on her bed, pressed her lips together, then stared fixedly out the window. ''I was busy.''

He didn't respond.

She sighed. ''I just felt weird about it, okay? I mean, we were...'' She made a vague gesture with her free hand. ''After that it would have been too strange. I've never kissed a doctor before.''

"What with our knowledge of anatomy, I'm sure we do it much better than untrained individuals."

She whipped her head around to glare at him. "Obviously your ego knows no boundaries at all."

"Probably not," he said cheerfully. "It's part of my charm."

"You're not the least bit charming."

"I'll ignore that, because we both know it's not true." He rose to his feet. "I'm going to fix you some weak tea. You can drink that until your mom arrives with the supplies." He started out of the room, and then paused. "I have to say, finding you like this has made me feel a lot better."

Her expression tightened. "What? You enjoy knowing I've been sick?"

"No, but I am pleased that the reason you didn't return my calls wasn't because you were avoiding me but because you were too ill to phone."

She reached behind her for a pillow. "You're a beast," she yelled as she tossed it toward him. "Go make my tea."

Chapter Six

Nora listened to Stephen rustling around in her kitchen. She told herself she should be furious with him, but she couldn't help a smile from tugging on the corners of her mouth. The man was annoying, difficult and, she hated to admit, completely charming. And handsome. His sandy-haired good looks were growing on her. She liked how his hazel eyes could look right through her facade. And the way his lean body moved. He had great hands and was a fabulous kisser. Worse—she wanted him.

Despite nearly a week of tossing her cookies every few hours, running a fever and generally feeling like something the cat had thrown up, she still felt a tingle of awareness just being around him. His examination had been completely professional and not the least bit intimate. Still, she'd felt herself melting. Of course the act of sticking the IV needle into her had squelched any romantic thoughts, she thought humorously. She looked at the bag of fluid slowly dripping into her system. She couldn't actually feel the liquid, although the needle wasn't the most comfortable sensation in the world. Still, it was both necessary and temporary. And it distracted her from thinking about Stephen, which was a good thing.

The last time they'd been together, he'd proposed an affair. A very adult relationship based on friendship and mutual attraction with no plan for anything lasting. Was he still interested in that, and if he was, what did *she* want? Her body ached for him—no question about that. But what about the rest of her? Could she disconnect her heart? She wasn't interested in falling in love with anyone, least of all him.

"Weak tea," Stephen announced as he walked back into her bedroom.

He set a mug on the nightstand. Next to it he settled a small plate with a single piece of dry toast. He nodded at the latter.

"Do the best you can with the toast," he said. "You don't have to eat yet if you're not ready, but I thought you might like to try."

She eyed the unappetizing square of bread. Her stomach felt hollow but she wasn't anxious to start throwing up again. "Maybe," she said doubtfully.

Stephen bent over her and collected pillows from the far side of the bed. Then he put one arm around her shoulders and drew her toward him. He shoved the extra pillows behind her, so she was more sitting than lying, then eased her back into place. Finally he handed her the mug.

"Drink," he ordered.

"Aren't you bossy," she complained before she took a sip.

He'd sweetened the dark liquid with honey. The taste was actually pleasant. She drank a bit more before resting the mug on her lap.

Stephen took the seat beside the bed and studied her. Nora shifted uneasily. "I'm not at my best," she said, stating the obvious.

"You're fine."

Oh. *Fine.* A word every woman longed to hear. "Darling, you look just fine." Except he hadn't said the darling part. Not that she wanted him to, she reminded herself. She wasn't interested in him or any man. She didn't get involved or do relationships.

She glanced at the gray slacks and dark blue shirt he wore under his white coat. "So did you abandon a waiting room full of patients to come see me?" she asked.

"No. I was finished for the day. Actually I was catching up on my journal reading. I was involved in a fascinating article on advances in the treatment of Lyme disease when I found out you were near death."

"I'm not near death. That was a couple of days ago." She paused. "Doesn't Lyme disease come from deer ticks?"

"Yes."

She shuddered. "Yuck. Who thinks this stuff up? I don't want to get ticks from deer. The idea of it makes me want to stay indoors for the rest of my life."

"But you're a Texan, Lord knows how many generations' worth. You grew up on a ranch. You should love being outside."

She looked at him over the rim of her mug. "You've been watching too much television. There's a reason I left the ranch when I turned eighteen. I love my family and I enjoy visiting on a regular basis, but I have no desire to live there again. Do you have any idea of the smells one encounters when working on a ranch?"

"I can't say I do."

"You're lucky."

He chuckled and leaned back in his chair, crossing his legs, resting one ankle on the opposite knee. "So you're not a barrel racer like your mother?"

Nora finished her tea and put the mug on the nightstand. She eyed the toast, but decided to wait for a bit before risking actual food in her stomach. "I did the junior rodeo thing when I was growing up. A lot of us did. But I never liked it very much. My mom wasn't one to push. After I tried for a couple of years, she let me stop. I always preferred getting dressed up to sprawling in the dirt."

"Did you always want to be a hairdresser?"

She glared at him, searching his expression to see if he was being sarcastic. "I know that setting someone's hair doesn't compare to saving a life, but it's what I do. I'm good at it."

He shook his head. "How about letting me mess up before you jump all over me. Quit assuming that I'm thinking the worst about you. Fair enough?"

"Maybe."

"Nora, you make me crazy." He sighed. "Tell me about your career. Is it what you always wanted to do? I'm asking because I'm interested."

She didn't exactly doubt his words, it was just that most men weren't entranced by what she did for a living. Snip 'n Clip was a foreign world to men and that frightened them.

"Yes, I always wanted to be a hairdresser. I started cutting my brothers' and sisters' hair when I was about twelve. I gave all my friends perms and highlights. I wasn't interested in college. I started beauty school when I was seventeen. It was a snap for me. When I graduated, I went to work in the Snip 'n Clip. I saved my money and eventually bought the place. I had a mortgage, but when they found oil on the ranch, Mom and Jack gifted everyone with a chunk of money. I used mine to pay off the bank. So the business is mine, free and clear."

"Not bad for someone who isn't even thirty."

She hadn't thought of it that way. "I guess you're right. I'm doing something I like, that makes people happy." She tilted her head and looked at him. "What about you? Are you sure you want to be a small-town doctor? Aren't you getting bored living here?"

He grinned. "Never. The longer I'm here, the more I know that this is where I belong. Lone Star Canyon is exactly the kind of place I was looking for."

She found herself wanting to believe that was true. But she couldn't imagine a man like him being happy here. "You said you spent the first few years practicing in an emergency room in Boston. Why did you change?"

A shadow drifted across his eyes, making her think that there were secrets in his past. Of course, everyone had secrets, although she couldn't think of any she had at the moment. Stephen already knew about David Fitzgerald dumping her practically the day before the wedding, and that was about as bad as it got in her world. But what about in Stephen's?

"I woke up one morning and realized I didn't want to go to work," he said quietly. "I didn't want to see twenty or thirty patients I would never treat again. I didn't mind the challenge of the different kinds of cases, but I hated that it was impersonal."

She sensed there was more, but she didn't ask. For one thing, it wasn't her place. For another, she was getting more and more tired. She tugged one of the pillows free so she was reclining on the bed.

"Did you always want to be a doctor?" she asked.

"From the time I was ten." He smiled at her. "It all started with my best friend, Jeff. He got cancer and had to go into the hospital. I visited him a lot. The medical staff was terrific, especially the doctors. They answered all our questions, even though we were just kids. Jeff got better and never wanted to see the inside of a hospital again, but I'd been hooked by the possibilities. I wanted to do for others what they had done for him."

Her eyelids felt impossibly heavy. "I might have to go to sleep now," she said, her voice sounding slightly slurred.

"It's the best thing for you."

"But my mom's not here yet."

"I'll let her in when she arrives."

"But you can't sit here while I sleep."

"Why not?"

She didn't have a good answer for that, but then she didn't have a good answer for much of anything right now. Her brain was mushy and thick.

Stephen shifted so that he was hovering over her.

He touched her forehead. "Your fever seems to be almost gone. I'm guessing the fluids are helping."

"It was the tea," she murmured, letting her eyelids sink all the way closed. "The best tea I've ever had."

"Thanks."

She turned on her side, toward him. "You're very nice."

"I try."

"Don't you want to kiss me good-night?"

He chuckled. "In your condition, I don't think it's a good idea."

"Because I look horrible?"

There was a pause. "You don't look horrible, Nora. You couldn't. You're an incredibly attractive, sexy woman. And you dress like a tease."

She smiled without opening her eyes. "I know. Isn't it fun?"

"Yes, and so are you."

Something warm brushed against her cheek. He'd kissed her, she thought in contentment. And then the world went dark.

By Friday Nora was back at work. Mrs. Arnold settled into the chair and smiled at her in the mirror.

"I heard that the good doctor made *several* house calls, making sure you were getting back on your feet."

Nora held back a sigh. It was barely ten-fifteen in the morning on her first day in the shop in nearly a week and the gossip was already starting. She shouldn't be surprised. It was one of the disadvantages of living in a small town. Little happened without an audience.

She reached for a brush and began smoothing the

elderly woman's white hair. "Dr. Remington was very kind," Nora said calmly. "I can't believe I didn't think I was sick enough to go see him on my own. If Jill hadn't insisted he make a house call, I don't know what would have happened."

She gave her co-worker a quick glance. Jill grinned. They were experts at diverting the attention of their "attentive" clientele.

She took a deep breath and continued before Mrs. Arnold could comment. "I think we often don't take the flu seriously enough. Didn't your sister end up in the hospital with pneumonia one year?" she asked.

Mrs. Arnold frowned. "Yes, she did. It was six years ago. Her bronchitis turned nasty. You know, it's not the flu that kills people, it's the secondary infections."

"I've heard that," Nora said, leading the woman to the back of the shop and the shampoo sinks.

"I remember when my grandmother had a bad case of the flu," Jill said helpfully. "I was very young at the time and I didn't know what was wrong with her."

Within ten minutes the shop was buzzing with flu recaps, symptom comparisons and horror stories about people who just wouldn't go see the doctor.

Mission accomplished, Nora thought with some relief. Although the topic was bound to come up again. The thought of the handsome, *single* doctor paying a single woman *daily* house calls was too much temptation for even the most discreet of souls. And when she was the single woman in question, there was no telling what people were saying. After all, she was the one with the reputation for being unapproachable where the male population was concerned.

Nora finished rolling Mrs. Arnold's white hair into tight rollers and settled her under a dryer. She returned to her station to check her supplies. But even as she counted clean towels and noted that she needed more hairspray, her gaze drifted until she found herself staring across the street at the medical offices. Was Stephen there even now? Was he thinking about her the way she kept finding herself thinking about him?

He'd been visiting her every day for the past four days, staying at least an hour, sometimes longer. He'd been funny, attentive, charming and completely professional. Not by a whisper or a glance had he allowed her to imagine he had anything but her health on his mind.

Which was a good thing, she told herself. He *should* take his job seriously. She was glad he'd been able to spend all that time with her and not think about sex or his ridiculous suggestion that they have an affair. If only she could have had the same self-control.

Because she'd been thinking about it plenty. Sometimes she told herself that she was crazy to even consider the idea. What was in it for her? Some good sex? A little companionship? So what? She didn't have either of those now and she was just fine. A woman like herself should be looking for...looking for...

Nora shook her head and forced herself to concentrate on the small cupboard next to her station. Supplies, she reminded herself. She was checking on supplies. As for what a woman like herself should be looking for—she didn't have a clue. Marriage? A happily-ever-after? She didn't think she was going to

get either this time around. Her father had broken her
heart when he'd left. It had taken her a long time to
figure out that his leaving didn't have anything to do
with her and that it was okay to trust another man not
to hurt her. Yet the very first man she'd given her
heart to again had dumped her publicly. Between her
past and all the awful stories she heard about men in
the salon, why on earth would she want to commit to
anything long term with any man? She was far better
off alone.

She straightened and headed for the supply room
at the rear of the salon. As she passed Jill's station,
she heard the other woman talking about her kids.

"They're both doing really well in school this
year," Jill was saying. "We spent most of last summer concentrating on their reading skills. It wasn't
easy at the time, but it's sure paid off. They're keeping up, doing their homework and getting it right, and
they both enjoy sitting down and reading a book
now."

Mrs. Arnold raised the hood of her dryer. "My
grandson Mark is at the top of his class," she said
proudly. "He's going to be applying to colleges next
year and his parents are talking about Harvard. Can
you imagine?"

"Oh, do you have a picture of Mark?" Kathy, one
of the stylists, asked. "I don't think I've seen a current one."

"In my purse." The older woman looked around
for her handbag.

Nora retrieved it from the closet and brought it to
her client. Mrs. Arnold showed the school picture of
her handsome teenage grandson to everyone. Soon

pictures were changing hands like cards at a poker game.

Nora participated by smiling and making appropriate remarks. But she didn't have any pictures of her own to pass around. Nor was she likely to. There was no husband, no children—not even any pets. As the other women talked about the people in their lives, she realized she was lonely and she'd been lonely for a long time.

Nora made a quick excuse and hurried to the rest room. Once there, she locked the door behind her and sank onto the small straight-backed chair in the corner. Lonely. Of course. Why hadn't she seen it before? All her friends were getting married and starting a family. Even her own brother was getting married. She was going to be thirty and she had to face the fact that if things continued the way they were now, she was going to live her life alone.

Nora sucked in a breath. She didn't mind not having a husband so much, but she ached at the thought of not having children. Somehow she'd always assumed she would be a mother.

Her chest tightened and the symptom had nothing to do with her recent illness. Sadness filled her. A deep, bone-chilling pain that made it difficult for her to keep from shivering. She tried to tell herself that there were other ways to have children. She didn't need a husband. She could adopt, or become a foster parent. She could go to a sperm bank, although to her mind that was a bit like ordering Chinese. Picking characteristics like so much moo shu chicken—one from column A, two from column B. But maybe, in a pinch.

She shook her head and rose to her feet. ''I don't

have time for this,'' she told herself. ''Not now.'' She had a customer under the dryer, a full day of appointments and a man who wanted to have an affair with her.

The latter was easy, she told herself. She'd decided what she would tell him. A simple, polite thanks but no thanks. She wasn't interested in what he was offering. They could be friends, but she wasn't willing to bother with anything else.

Nora's resolve lasted right up until Stephen Remington walked into her shop at six-fifteen that evening. All of her employees had already left and her last customer had paid and was slipping on a sweater before leaving. Normally the shop stayed open late on Fridays, but there was a big high school basketball game that everyone wanted to get to.

Stephen breezed in as if the Snip 'n Clip was a second home to him. He nodded at her customer, held open the door like a real gentleman, then gave Nora a devastatingly sexy smile.

''How are you feeling?'' he asked.

''Fine.''

She offered a bright smile of her own, all the while doing her best to ignore the fluttering in the region of her heart and the way that her palms suddenly felt damp. It was either a strong reaction to his presence or a relapse of the flu. She had a feeling that she wasn't going to be lucky enough to be getting the flu again.

''It's your first day back,'' he said. ''I hope you didn't overdo it.''

''Me? No. I'm fine.''

He leaned against the front counter. ''I wanted to

check on you because I've gotten used to seeing you every day.''

Her throat went dry as her thighs seemed to heat up alarmingly. Was it her or had the temperature in the room just about doubled? And why did he have to look so darned cute in his chinos and light blue shirt? He was tall, good-looking, and she had the strongest urge to throw herself against him.

Nora hurried toward the rear of the shop where she collected a broom and dustpan. She returned to her station and swept up the hair on the floor. What had happened to her resolve? Hadn't she just that morning promised herself that she didn't want anything to do with Stephen or his ridiculous proposition? Sex for sex's sake. How insane. Except with her body all aquiver, it didn't seem quite as crazy as she'd hoped.

"I did have a full day," she admitted, careful to not look at him. "But I gave myself several breaks. I'm a little tired, but nothing horrible. I plan to make it an early evening. A light dinner and then into bed for me."

Bed? Argh! Why did she have to say the ''b'' word? She emptied the dustpan into the trash and returned it and the broom to the corner.

He straightened and walked toward her. "Nora, we have to talk." He reached out to touch her arm.

The second his fingers grazed her skin, she felt all her resolve giving way. In that second she knew she could deny him nothing. Not even when her good sense told her otherwise. Obviously she couldn't trust herself to say no, so she had to keep him from asking.

"I had been a little concerned," she said, neatly stepping around him and hurrying to the front of the shop. Once there she pulled the shades. At least their discussion wouldn't be witnessed by anyone walking by.

"Concerned?"

"You know, about being weak from being sick. But it wasn't bad at all. We received a shipment for a new perm solution while I was gone. I used it for the first time today. I think it's going to work well."

She turned and saw him walking purposefully toward her. Panic set in. She began straightening magazines in the waiting area. "Hasn't the weather been terrific? Spring is kind of iffy around here. It can be warm and clear, but we also get those huge storms blowing in. That's what caused the tornado. Oh, speaking of which, how's that guy? The one in the back of the truck? Remember, he had that really deep cut and I was wondering if—"

He took her in his arms and pressed his mouth to hers. She tried to resist him. Really. But the second his lips brushed hers, she had all the resolve of a marshmallow.

He didn't even kiss her long. Just a few seconds of contact. When he drew back she was out of breath and hungry. She wanted to throw herself into his embrace and beg him to take her right there.

"We have to talk," he repeated.

"No." She swallowed hard and tried to summon up a little backbone. "This is a really bad idea. We have nothing in common. You're a doctor and I do hair."

He frowned. "What does that have to do with anything? I don't care what you do for a living. You're smart as a whip and if anyone is at risk of feeling inadequate in this relationship, it's me. We get along.

We can talk about anything. I think you're funny, not to mention sexy as hell. So what's the problem?''

She liked what he was saying, but she refused to let herself be swayed. "We could never have a real relationship."

He still held on to her arms. Now he rubbed his thumbs up and down, sliding under her short sleeves and making her shiver. "Is that what you want? A traditional relationship?"

She hesitated. "Not really. I don't think many of them work."

"I don't want that, either. I don't want to fall in love or worry about getting married. What I want is something special *with* someone special. I've never been into quantity, so I'm not interested in sleeping around. I *am* interested in being your lover, however. I'd like that very much. I think we could have a great time, both in and out of bed. I promise to be monogamous, attentive and always make it good for you. I'd like us to be friends, doing things together. And when this dies a natural death, I would like us to be able to walk away without any hard feelings."

Her brain didn't seem able to absorb all he was saying. "You make it sound so rational," she said, not sure what she wanted. All she knew was that her body had never been on fire like this before. She'd thought she'd experienced passion before, but she'd been wrong. And if it was like this after a simple, chaste kiss, what would happen if they did the wild thing for real?

"It *is* rational. Say yes."

Before she could figure out what she wanted to say, he was kissing her again. But this time the contact was far from chaste. Even as his mouth came down on hers, one of his hands slid to her rear, while the other settled on her breast. When she gasped in shock, his tongue slid into her mouth.

They surged against each other. His fingers cupped her full curves, top and bottom. Instantly desire swept through her, making her knees buckle. She had to cling to him to keep from falling. Their tongues circled each other. The exquisite stroking was better than the last time. Perhaps because she knew what to expect. Every part of her was on fire. They couldn't do this. She had to make him stop. She had to—

He teased her nipple. Tension raced through her until she was afraid she might actually climax. Her muscles tensed in anticipation. He shifted and wrapped both arms around her, hauling her against him. His arousal jutted against her belly.

He wanted her as much as she wanted him. How was she supposed to resist that?

She pulled back and stared at him. Passion darkened his eyes. His breathing was as fast as her own.

"I don't think I can survive not having you," he said, his voice low and hoarse.

She nodded. "Your place or mine?"

Chapter Seven

Nora pulled the sweater over her head and shoved her arms into the sleeves. As she straightened the garment, she kept glancing at the clock. Less than twenty minutes, she thought, trying not to panic. Stephen would be here in less than twenty minutes. It wasn't nearly enough time to get everything done, but it was more than enough time for her to have about a million second thoughts.

Her place, he'd said in answer to her breathless question of where they were to go next. Her place and he would give her an hour to get ready. When he'd spoken the words, an hour had seemed endless, but now she knew there would never be enough time for her to prepare.

She looked at her reflection in the mirror and frowned. What exactly did one wear to begin an affair? She wanted to appear sexy but not obvious, accessible without being easy. Clothes lay in crumpled heaps at her feet. She'd tried on nearly everything in her closet and nothing seemed right. Not to mention that she really hated this sweater.

She jerked it over her head and tossed it on the floor with the other rejects. Clad only in a peach-colored bra and panties that she'd ordered from a ridiculously expensive catalog, she studied the rest of the clothes still in her closet.

The man was visiting her for the express purpose of having sex. When she'd offered to cook something, he'd informed her that he wasn't interested in any meal that didn't include her. Remembering the words sent a shiver up her spine. She glanced at the clock. Fifteen minutes. Damn.

She reached in blindly and pulled out a cream-colored knit dress that buttoned up the front. It was short, fitted and left little to the imagination. Nora tilted her head to study the dress, then nodded. No point in being subtle. Two minutes later she had the dress buttoned just high enough to cover the front clasp of her bra. She grabbed a brush and ran it through her hair, then dabbed perfume on the inside of her elbows.

A couple of well-aimed kicks sent the piles of clothes on the floor into the closet. She shoved the door closed, then studied her bedroom. She'd put on fresh sheets that morning. There were probably too many pillows and frills for Stephen's taste, but that couldn't be helped. There wasn't anything embarrassing left out on the dresser or nightstand. Good.

She hurried out of the bedroom and made a beeline for the kitchen. From the refrigerator she pulled out a bottle of white wine. She dug out the ice bucket, filled it with ice, then plopped the wine inside. Seldom used wineglasses had to be dusted before she put them on a tray and set the ice bucket next to it. She carried the tray into the living room. There was just enough time to sweep several days' worth of newspapers into a corner behind the club chair, when someone knocked on her door.

She jumped, her heart rising in her throat. He was here. Now what?

"B-be right there," Nora said, hating the faint shudder in her voice. She wanted to come off as coolly sophisticated, which is exactly the opposite of how she felt. She knew that she'd been crazy to agree to Stephen's proposal. She could no more pull this off than she could develop a rocket capable of space flight to another galaxy. She would have to explain that to Stephen…just as soon as she gathered the courage to let him in.

She paused by the front door and smoothed her hair. She'd opted for minimal makeup and no lipstick. Now she tugged on her dress, glanced down at her bare feet and wondered if she should have worn shoes, then swallowed hard and opened the door.

Stephen stood on her front porch. He'd changed into jeans and a white shirt. He was tall, lean and too handsome for words. He was also holding a huge spray of yellow roses. Her heart left her throat and plunged for her toes. She found herself unable to breathe, which didn't really matter. He was a doctor and could easily revive her.

"I took a chance on the flowers," he said as he stepped into the house and handed her the bouquet. "I thought it might be too much of a cliché, but when I saw them, I couldn't resist."

She inhaled the heady fragrance. "The yellow rose of Texas?"

"Something like that."

She clutched the flowers in her arms, feeling a bit like a runner-up in a beauty pageant. "They're beautiful. Thanks. I should probably put them in water. While I'm doing that, why don't you pour us some wine?" She freed one hand long enough to motion to the tray she'd set up on the coffee table.

Instead of moving, Stephen grinned at her. "Do you need to be drunk to do this?"

"No, but it might help me relax."

"You're nervous?"

She thought about rolling her eyes while muttering "Well, duh!" but didn't think either action was especially mood-setting. "Just a little," is what she managed to say instead.

"Then maybe we should get right to it," he said, moving close, taking the flowers from her and dropping them onto the sofa. "Then you'll have less time to think."

"You want to do it now?" She winced at the outrage in her voice. She cleared her throat. "What I meant is maybe we should talk, drink wine, relax."

Without shoes, she barely came as high as his nose. Which meant he could do something really irritating, like drop a kiss on her forehead.

"You're not going to relax until this is over," he said, leaning against the back of the sofa and drawing her between his thighs. "Your muscles are tight and I can tell you're trembling." He rested his hands on her waist. "Have you changed your mind?"

They were standing really close. Their legs were touching, and if she leaned toward him, even just a little, they were going to be touching from belly to shoulder. Is that what she wanted?

Without thinking about what she was doing, she pressed her palms flat against his broad chest. He felt warm, muscled and very masculine. Nice, actually. The passion that had stirred in her shop when he'd kissed her returned to life. Need began to flare inside of her.

She slid her hands up to his shoulders and allowed herself to drift forward until her nipples teased his shirt. Delicious sensations shot through her. She wanted to have him touch her breast again, the way he had at the shop. But this time she wanted them both naked. She wanted to feel his skin against hers, his body, hard and ready, plunging into her.

The edges of the room seemed to swim out of focus. She felt herself sway slightly as heat flared between her legs. Her bones began melting. So why didn't the man kiss her? What exactly was he waiting for?

"Nora?"

"Hmm?"

"Did you plan on answering my question?"

"Huh?" There'd been a question? "What did you want to know?"

"Have you changed your mind?"

She blinked slowly, staring deeply into Stephen's hazel eyes. He had lovely eyes. Reflections of the soul, isn't that what they said?

"About you kissing me?" She was confused. "No, I want you to. Sooner would be better."

"No." His voice sounded patient, although a little strained. "Do you still want to make love?"

"Of course. What do you think we've been talking about?"

"Hell if I know," he grumbled, then claimed her mouth with his.

He'd kissed her before—outside in her driveway and at her shop. Both times she'd found herself weak with desire. But this kiss was different. Maybe because they were alone and in private. Maybe it was because they were starting to know each other. Maybe it was just hormones coming out to play for the first time in years. Regardless, Nora found herself being swept away by a passion that left her breathless.

She tilted her head and opened to let him kiss her deeply. As his tongue entered her mouth, she stroked him, rubbing and circling, wanting him to learn all of her. They played tag and chase until she followed him back and learned all of his secrets. His sweet taste made her want to know the flavors of all of him. His neck, his shoulders, his belly—that most private part of him. Later, she thought hazily, wrapping her arms around him and pulling him even closer. Time for all that later.

As they kissed he moved his hands up and down her back. On one of the trips he moved lower, down past her rear, then slipped under her dress as he moved back up. He cupped her rear and squeezed, drawing her against him, letting her feel the hardness of his arousal. The realization that he wanted her as much as she wanted him nearly made her cry out in pleasure. Need filled her, increasing in time with her rapidly beating heart.

He slipped his fingers under the elastic of her pants and caressed the bare skin of her behind. The light touch tickled as much as it aroused, making her squirm. Then his hands were on her waist and moving higher. Up her rib cage to her breasts. He didn't even pause. Instead he brought both hands up under her curves, then closed around them and squeezed gently.

The sensation was exquisite. She'd forgotten how good it could all feel. The heat of a man, him touching her body. But this wasn't just about being without, she thought as his thumbs and forefingers teased her nipples. This was about being specifically with Stephen—the man who had forced his way past her emotional walls and reminded her that she was a vital, sensual woman.

He broke the kiss and rested his forehead against hers. "You've got me way too close," he breathed. "And neither of us is naked." He kissed her cheeks, her nose, her chin, then nibbled along her throat. All the while his fingers continued to caress her breasts.

"You feel so good," he continued, licking her collarbone, then slipping down to dip into the valley between her breasts. "I want to touch all of you. I want to see you and be inside of you." He raised his head and smiled. "Maybe we should continue this in your bedroom."

"I'd like that," she whispered.

Passion darkened his eyes. He cupped her face and kissed her softly, then took her hand and led the way down the hall.

Once they were in her bedroom, he turned toward her and began unfastening her dress. She was surprised to realize that his fingers shook and he could barely manage the small buttons. She'd been so busy worrying about her own case of nerves that she hadn't considered he might be feeling the same.

When he stalled on the third button, she pushed his

hands away. "I can finish this. Why don't you take off your shirt?"

They worked in tandem until she finished and shrugged off the dress. It fell to the floor, leaving her in her peach bra and matching bikini panties. Stephen froze in the act of unfastening his shirt. She saw the hard ridge pressing against the fly of his slacks flex, as if more heated blood had surged into place.

Nora had never thought much about her body. She'd been blessed with a good gene pool and a tendency to stay slim easily. She dressed the way she liked and didn't care about other people's opinion. But when Stephen stared at her like a hungry man seeing food for the first time in weeks, she felt a ripple of pleasure tingling through her. When he swore and reached for her, she was thrilled that he was pleased.

"You're incredible," he murmured, before claiming her mouth.

She wrapped her arms around him and drew him against her. His hands were everywhere. Along her bare back, at her hips, her rear, sliding up and down her sides. He traced the back of her bra, then followed the material around to unfasten the front hook. She slipped off the scrap of fabric.

He stopped kissing her long enough to stare at her full curves. Then he groaned as he took them in his hands. "Perfect," he told her as he bent down to lick her taut nipples.

The feel of his tongue on her aroused skin was nearly enough to send her to her knees. She had to cling to him to keep herself from falling. When he drew her nipple into his mouth and sucked, she gasped and clutched his head. Fiery need shot through her. Desperate passion flamed in her belly and lower. With each tug of his mouth she felt an answering response between her legs.

"Don't stop," she breathed.

Without releasing her, he urged her backward until she felt the bed against her legs. Stephen straightened and jerked out of his shirt. Then he picked her up in his arms and tumbled her onto the bed.

She came down on the soft mattress, just as he settled next to her. Then his mouth was on her breasts again and she knew she was going to die from the wonder of it all.

He licked her, circled, gently nibbled, all the while matching his actions with his hand on her other breast. He returned his mouth to hers and trailed a hand down her belly to the elastic of her panties.

She knew what he was going to do and tried to brace herself for the impact. But it wasn't enough. Even as he slipped under the scrap of silk, she felt herself tensing.

"How do you like it?" he asked, barely whispering in her ear. "Soft? Slow? Fast?" He moved as he spoke, demonstrating the possibilities.

She couldn't pick one of them, she thought frantically. They all felt incredible. "It doesn't matter," she breathed.

He paused long enough to pull off her panties. Then he returned his fingers to her waiting heat and brushed against her most sensitive spot. Back and forth, up and down, circling, brushing, arousing until she couldn't do anything but focus on that single place of perfection.

"So ready," he whispered as he licked the inside of her ear. "You're so amazingly sexy. I want you. I swear if you touched me, I would explode in about a second. I can't wait to be inside of you. I want to fill you and feel you lose control.''

His words painted an erotic picture she couldn't resist. Her knees fell open and her hips arched into his touch. She was getting closer, she could feel it.

And then she couldn't stop herself. Her need for release grew until she was so tightly strung that she thought she might snap. She couldn't breathe, couldn't talk, couldn't do anything but hang suspended in one incredible moment of anticipation.

''You're close,'' he whispered. ''I can feel it.''

He shifted slightly, pressing his thumb against her secret place and dipping a finger into her waiting passage. It was too much. Pleasure poured through her in waves of light and heat. Her muscles tensed and pulsed over and over again until she was trembling and gasping and very near to tears. He touched her lightly until the end, then he wrapped his arms around her and held her close.

''You're incredible,'' he said.

She managed a weak smile. ''Imagine how it will be when we're both involved.''

''I already have.''

He kissed her lightly before standing up and quickly removing his shoes, socks, jeans and briefs. Before joining her back on the bed, he reached for his jeans and removed a condom from the front pocket.

Nora had been busy admiring the lean strength of his legs and the way the hair on his belly arrowed down toward his jutting arousal. Now her gaze settled on the protection he held. Her brain froze.

''I'd forgotten,'' she admitted, more to herself than

him. "I'm not on any birth control and I never gave it a moment's thought. It's been a long time and—"

Stephen slid back onto the mattress and brushed his mouth against hers. "I wasn't sure. It seemed easier to be safe."

She settled back on her pillow and ran her fingers up and down his chest. "I should have known those years of medical training would pay off sometime."

"My thoughts exactly. Now, where were we?"

Before she could answer, he'd slid on the protection, then moved over her, kissing first her mouth, then her breasts. She felt herself quickly readying again. She was hot and eager to feel him inside of her.

He knelt between her thighs. She felt the first stretching pressure as he gently pushed into her. Her legs parted more and she put her hands on the small of his back to draw him inside. Slowly, deeply, wonderfully, he filled her until she couldn't imagine anything more amazing than sharing this physical intimacy with him.

He groaned as he thrust in again. His passion-filled gaze met hers. "I can't hold back very long. I want to, it's just…"

She smiled. "That's hardly an insult. Besides, I'm not going to take very long myself."

Already she could feel her body tensing in readiness. With each thrust he drew her closer and closer to the place of release.

Slipping his arms around her, he bent down and kissed her. Tongues mirrored the act of love they performed. She wrapped her arms around him, drawing him in more deeply, taking all of him, surging against each thrust in a rhythm that forced her over the edge.

She cried out her release. Seconds later he stiffened and gasped her name. They held each other tightly as they rode out the storm.

Stephen leaned back in the kitchen chair, contentment filling him. Making love with Nora had been better than he'd imagined. She'd not only been beautiful and sexy, she'd been the most responsive female he'd ever encountered. The way she'd climaxed... both times. He'd thought it would be good—he hadn't dared to hope it would be amazing.

"What are you thinking?" she asked as she glanced up from the counter where she worked.

He'd found the energy to pull on jeans, but nothing else. She was dressed in a white terry-cloth robe that should have looked sensible, but was instead about the sexiest thing he'd ever seen a woman wear. Just watching the thick collar part slightly and show a hint of bare breast was enough to get him hard again. Of course, he figured Nora would make him hard doing just about anything.

"I think you're amazing," he said, coming to his feet and moving behind her.

She was making them sandwiches. He hugged her, tucking both his hands into the robe and gently squeezing her breasts. Her nipples puckered instantly.

"I can't work while you're doing that," she said calmly. "Do you want food or sex?"

"Do I have to pick just one? Can't we do both?"

"Yes, but not together. Earlier you said you weren't interested in food, but a few minutes ago you said you were starving. Which is it?"

He buried his face in her sweet-smelling hair and sighed. "Can we eat now and make love later?"

Her slight shiver in response to his words made him smile.

"Sure," she told him.

Reluctantly he returned to the table. She continued to fix the sandwiches, then dug some potato salad out of the refrigerator and put a scoop on each of their plates.

Stephen walked into the living room and retrieved the wine and the flowers. He felt good—better than he had in a long time. Even though he'd wanted to make love with Nora, he'd wondered if he would have any problems being intimate with another woman. A part of him had been concerned that thoughts of Courtney would interfere.

But he hadn't thought of her at all. Instead he'd found himself intoxicated by the wonder that was Nora. He was pleased to know that he could experience physical lovemaking without feeling guilty.

He opened the wine and poured them each a glass. Nora set the food on the table, then arranged the roses in a vase. She took the seat across from him and picked up her sandwich.

Her skin was still flushed, her mouth swollen. Her curly, dark hair tumbled over her shoulders. She looked like a woman who had just spent the afternoon in bed. He found himself wanting her again, needing to be with her. He wanted to learn her secrets, hear about her past, explore what they had in common and what was different.

A warning sounded in his head. Friends, he reminded himself. Lovers. All that was fine, but not *in love.* Never in love.

"So," Nora said after swallowing her first bite of

food. "Why isn't a halfway decent guy like you married?"

Her question made him laugh. "Trust you to get right to the point. No subtleties, no gently leading to the question. Just down and dirty. Why aren't you married?"

"Are you avoiding the question?"

"Not at all. I'm just wondering why you think I would be."

She rolled her eyes at him. "Oh, please. You're fishing for compliments, which seems so beneath you. We've established that you're practically good-looking, almost intelligent and you have a somewhat successful career."

He sipped his wine. "I'm overwhelmed by your flattery."

Humor brightened her eyes. "You should be. So there must be at least a half dozen or so women who would think of you as a catch of some kind."

"But not you?"

She arched her eyebrows. "Do you really want to go there?"

"Not really." He leaned toward her. "Okay. I'll confess. I was married once."

She set down her sandwich and slapped her hands on the table. "I knew it. You see—this just proves my theory. It's the reason you're divorced. You see, my theory is that every man has a hideous flaw. Some drink, some gamble, some are mean, some complete slobs. Whatever. The trick to a successful marriage is for the woman to find out the man's hideous flaw *before* they get hitched and figure out if she can live with it."

How Nora-like, he thought wryly. "Do you have a theory for everything?"

"Just about."

"There's just one problem."

She held up her hand. "I know what you're going to say. You want to know if women also have hideous flaws. Some do, I'll admit, but the majority manage to stay hideously flaw-free. I am one of those fortunate women."

"Of course," he murmured. "Why would I think otherwise?"

She propped her chin on her hand and smiled. "So, lover of mine. Tell me about your hideous flaw. What broke up the marriage?"

"Nothing." He shrugged. "That's what I was trying to tell you. I'm not divorced. I'm a widower."

Chapter Eight

Nora was having an out-of-body experience. Instead of participating in the conversation with Stephen, she was floating in a corner of the kitchen. She could see herself, sitting at the table, looking shocked but interested. He was talking and talking, but she couldn't hear a word.

A widower? Stephen?

She blinked and found herself planted firmly on her chair, struggling to act normal when she wasn't able to breathe or think or understand anything. He'd been in love with his wife and then she'd died, leaving him alone and mourning?

She wasn't sure why the thought was so shocking. People lost spouses. Although it was usually the husband who died first, sometimes it was the wife.

"But she must have been so young," she said, interrupting him in midsentence.

''She was,'' he agreed. ''Thirty-four. Courtney was a year older than me.''

Courtney. Nora repeated the name over silently. ''She sounds pretty and petite.''

A soft smile pulled at the corner of his mouth. ''She was. Damn smart, too. Always at the top of her class. She was a brilliant surgeon with almost magical hands. She was intuitively connected with her patients. At least that's what her teachers always said.''

Courtney sounded like a paragon, Nora thought grimly. A tiny, perfect doll of a woman who could save the world. And a doctor. Of course. ''Did you meet in medical school?''

''Yes.'' He took a bite of his sandwich and chewed. ''She was a couple of years ahead of me. That was partly because of the year age difference, but she'd also graduated from college when she was sixteen. She'd skipped a grade early on. Her specialty required years and years of training, and she used to say she wanted to be out and practicing before she turned forty.''

Nora knew she was going to hate herself for asking, but she couldn't help herself. ''What *was* her specialty?''

''Pediatric neurosurgery.''

She pushed her plate away and reached for her wine. ''Of course,'' she murmured. A brilliant, beautiful woman who devoted her life to saving children. But not just as a pediatrician. No, that would be too simple.

She tugged at the collar of her robe, wishing she didn't feel quite so naked and vulnerable. Not to mention stupid. Nora knew that she was smarter than most. She had a quick brain and a mouthy attitude that had never let her down. But facts were facts. She was a hairdresser from a tiny town in Texas. She had a high school education along with a couple of night courses in managing a small business. She could hold her own with most people she knew, but not with a brilliant and gifted surgical saint.

"Courtney and I met through mutual friends at a study session," Stephen was saying. "She and I started talking one afternoon and things progressed from there. We were married the summer after I graduated from medical school."

"Your family must have been thrilled—their son the doctor marrying another doctor."

She was doing her best to try to sound vaguely normal. Stephen's quick, questioning glance told her she might not be succeeding.

"They were happy enough," he said.

"I'm sure."

She cleared her throat. What was she supposed to say now? She was sorry she'd opened the line of inquiry to begin with, but now she was stuck with the topic. She might as well find out everything all at once.

"How, um, long were you married?"

"Nearly seven years. We were living in Boston. Courtney had just started a fellowship when we found out she was pregnant."

Nora had been drinking her wine, but at his latest announcement, she nearly spit. At the last minute, she was able to control herself. Unfortunately the liquid went down the wrong way and she started choking.

"Are you all right?" he asked, half rising to his feet.

She motioned him back into his chair as she continued to cough. "Fine," she managed to say in a slightly wheezy, strangled voice. "Go on."

Stephen hesitated. "The timing wasn't the greatest for Courtney," he said. "The baby, I mean. She'd been hoping to get the fellowship and it meant lots of extra hours of work. Unfortunately the pregnancy was physically difficult for her."

She sensed there was more to the story, but Nora wasn't about to ask for details. She'd heard about all the truth she could handle. The small amount of food she'd eaten felt like rocks in the pit of her stomach. She didn't want to know any more; she already knew too much. That Stephen had been married before, and that his perfect, beautiful doctor wife had had a baby.

The thought of a child made her heart ache. A baby of her own. Nora longed for children, although the details of having one had yet to be worked out. Being a single parent in the rest of the country might be acceptable, but it was still shocking behavior in Lone Star Canyon. Besides, she didn't as a rule have intimate relations with many men. Which meant the old-fashioned way of fathering wasn't going to work for her. She'd yet to work up the nerve to pursue other options, although she had considered adoption.

"Courtney miscarried in her seventh month."

Stephen's flat statement drew her back to the conversation already in progress. She stared at him, not able to believe what she'd heard. "She lost the baby?"

He nodded. "I was working a double shift, and by the time I found out there was a problem and got to the hospital, the baby was already gone. Courtney had died as well."

Pain darkened his hazel eyes, although he spoke

lightly enough. "So those are all my deep, dark secrets. Probably not as exciting as you thought."

She knew that he was trying to lighten the mood, but she couldn't play along. Not when she was still trying to absorb all he'd said. "You must have been very happy together," she murmured. "Courtney sounds like a wonderful woman."

"She was everything I'd ever wanted and I loved her very much. It's been over two years since she died. The first year I was numb. Then I started healing and realized that I wanted to return to my dream of being a country doctor. Which is how I ended up here."

She gave him a slight smile because she didn't know what to say. How did one respond to all that information? Courtney was so different from anyone Nora had ever met...most especially Stephen's late wife was different from Nora herself.

She risked another sip of wine. "Why me?"

He raised his eyebrows and grinned. "You mean why did I allow myself to be seduced by a beautiful face and an even more enticing body?"

His compliments didn't make her feel any better. "Something like that."

"I was lonely," he said, leaning toward her. "You are beautiful and sexy, but you're also something of a challenge. I appreciate that, Nora. I haven't dated much since I lost Courtney. In fact you're the first one I've been with...in every sense of the word."

She wasn't sure if that was good or bad. She tugged at her robe again, wishing she'd taken the time to put on her clothes so she wouldn't have to feel so naked in front of him.

"I appreciate being your springboard back to the

dating scene,'' she said. ''Now that you have your feet wet and realize that you still have what it takes, you can get on with seducing all the single women in Lone Star Canyon.''

''Is that what you think I'm interested in? Volume? Besides, I'd like to point out that most of the single women in this town are either under twenty or over sixty-five.''

''So it was me or nothing?''

She wished she could call the words back, but she couldn't. Stephen looked at her quizzically. ''Nora, what's wrong?''

''Nothing. It's just, I don't know. Strange.''

''Knowing about my past?''

She picked up her plate of barely touched food and carried it to the sink. ''Yes. Of course. I thought it would be different.''

She stood facing her sink. She heard him moving, and then he was standing behind her, wrapping his arms around her, pulling her back against him.

''Why does it change anything? I meant what I said. I really enjoy being with you. Neither of us is looking for a long-term commitment. You've made your feelings about men and marriage very clear and I don't want to go through all that again. We're perfect for each other.''

''I guess.''

But she wasn't convinced. Nor could she explain why she felt so...so...*betrayed*. She just knew things would have been easier if Stephen had been divorced. If he'd fallen out of love with his wife and left her, or even been left. But losing his wife and his baby because they'd died was worse somehow.

Plus now she knew for sure he meant what he said

about not wanting a serious relationship. He was in this for the sex. She didn't doubt his claim to monogamy, but she knew that he wasn't about to fall in love anytime soon. At least not with her. Not that she wanted him to. She didn't do love and marriage. She'd been burned enough, thank you very much.

Stephen continued to hold Nora. While an hour before, when they'd been making love, she'd been yielding and available, now he felt as if she'd emotionally gone away for the night. Her body was stiff, her comments stilted. If he didn't know better, he would say he'd hurt her. Except he couldn't have. The information about his past might have surprised her, but it shouldn't have had an impact on her.

Had he made a mistake in talking about Courtney? He didn't usually share what had happened to him, but telling Nora had been easy. He not only liked and respected her; he trusted her. Was she afraid he was still caught up in loving his wife? Should he try to explain that he'd made peace with the past? That while he would always love Courtney, he was ready to move on?

"Is something wrong?" he asked. "Are you angry or hurt?"

She shook her head. "Of course not."

He noticed that despite her claims to the contrary, she didn't bother turning to face him. Not that staring at the back of her head didn't have its advantages. While he loved looking at her perfect face, he also enjoyed the curve of her rear pressing against his groin. Being this close to her, holding her, was more than enough to make him hard.

He pulled her hair off her neck. "So if you're not upset, you won't mind me doing this."

He brushed his lips against her exposed skin, then licked where he'd kissed. A shiver rippled through her.

"I want you," he breathed, then turned her in his arms so that he could take her mouth.

For a heartbeat or two, she didn't respond. Her arms hung loosely at her sides and her body didn't press against his. But as he deepened the kiss, brushing his tongue against hers and rubbing his arousal against her stomach, he felt the quivering beginning of her desire. Her arms came around him. Her fingers touched the back of his head, then tunneled into his hair, drawing him closer. He felt the heat of her through the thick fabric of her robe as her hips arched against him.

His heartbeat thundered in his ears. He felt more than heard the answering echo from her body as blood ran hot and need filled them until they were caught in an erotic frenzy.

He reached for the ties on her robe and jerked them open with one quick tug. Before she could respond, he slipped the garment off her shoulders, exposing her naked body to him. He broke the kiss so that he could look at her—the fullness of her breasts, the sweep of her hip, the graceful curve of her legs. Color stained her cheeks—embarrassment from his bold appraisal—but she didn't back away or cover herself.

"You're magnificent," he told her, taking her hand and leading her to a chair by the table. He urged her to sit, then he sank to his knees and pressed a kiss to her flat belly.

"What did you have in mind?" she asked, but the light in her eyes told him that she not only knew— she approved.

Instead of answering, he gave her a slow smile, then dropped a trail of kisses along her right thigh. As he nibbled the scented, sweet flesh there, he rubbed his palms up and down her shins. He tickled the skin at the back of her knees, then traced the sleek line of her outer thigh.

Her legs fell open at his touch. He grasped her hips and pulled her toward him. As he slid his hands up to her hips, then higher still to her breasts, he bent low and kissed her most feminine place.

Just one kiss, he told himself, even as he knew he was lying. He was going to do much more than kiss her. He was going to make love to her intimately, lovingly, tasting her, pleasing her until she screamed his name and he went mad from needing her. Already the hunger grew inside of him. His own arousal flexed and throbbed in time with his heart. If she'd reached down and touched him, he would have lost control in a nanosecond. Fortunately she was too busy holding on to the chair to pay any attention to him.

He stroked her with his tongue. He easily found the spot of her pleasure, the knot of nerves that allowed him to take her to paradise and back. As he circled that sensitive spot with his tongue, he used his fingers to tease and caress her breasts. He cupped the heavy curves, then stroked her tight nipples. Her breath caught, her body shuddered and still he continued to have his way with her.

He dropped his hands to her hips and pulled her forward again, this time shifting so that her thighs were up over his shoulders and she was completely exposed to him. She had to grasp the sides of the seat to keep her balance. Her breathing came in tight pants and she made little moaning sounds in the back of her throat. Every breath, every noise heightened his own passion. He was torn between wanting to prolong the moment and the desperate need to plunge himself deep inside of her.

He sucked in a breath and forced himself to stay in control of his desires. Instead of thinking of the aching pressure between his legs, he returned his attention to Nora's exquisite body and the pleasure he could give her. He slipped a single finger into her waiting warmth even as he began stroking her intimately again. He moved faster and lighter, sensing the building pressure inside of her.

Tiny contractions massaged his finger. His tongue moved over that small bump in a gentle, steady movement. He shifted, slipping a second finger inside, stretching her slightly. He pressed up, rubbing her from the inside. In and out, back and forth. She quivered and shook and called out his name. Still the tension grew. With his free hand, he reached up and brushed against her tight nipple.

She screamed.

Her muscles began to contract around his fingers. Her legs trembled violently and she clutched at his head, holding him to her. As pleasure poured through her, intense satisfaction poured through him. He'd *wanted* to make her scream and cry and cling. He wanted to learn everything about her body so that he could reduce her to a puddle with just a look. She was the most amazingly erotic woman he'd ever known.

At last her release slowed and he straightened. Her legs slid down until her feet touched the ground. She opened her eyes and smiled at him. He kissed her thigh, but kept his fingers inside of her, still moving in and out, slow at first, but gaining in speed.

"You can't be serious," she complained. "There's no way you're going to make me do that again. You should just do your thing and be satisfied knowing you've reduced me to a limp rag."

"I don't think so," he said, locking his gaze with hers. "I prefer our lovemaking to be mutual. I want you."

His words made her pupils dilate slightly. Goose bumps erupted on her skin. He bent forward and took her nipple in his mouth.

"I can't," she whispered. "Not again. I've never been one to do that more than once."

He looked up at her. "What about earlier?"

"I have no explanation for that."

"Then let's see if we can do it again."

Even as she shook her head to protest, he felt her tighten around his finger. He kept up the steady rhythm until she was breathing heavily.

"I can't believe you're doing this to me," she said between gasps.

"Me, neither."

He stood up and pulled her to her feet. He was too ready, too needy to wait until they got to the bedroom. Instead he set the last plate on the chair she'd vacated and urged her onto the table. As she shifted into position, parting her legs for him, he unfastened his jeans and quickly pulled on a condom.

"You're not even taking off your pants?" she teased, even as she guided him into her.

"No time," he gasped as he plunged into her.

She opened her mouth to say something else, but a sudden spasm cut off her words. He felt as well as saw the release surge through her, making her cling to him and shudder, sucking him in deeper and making it impossible for him to do anything but surrender in return.

Two more quick thrusts forced him over the edge. Pressure built, then gave way as his pure pleasure filled him. He, in turn, held on to her, breathing in the scent of her, glorying in the perfection of their sexual match.

They hugged each other close until their breathing returned to normal. Finally Nora pulled back a little and smiled. "I'll never be able to look at this table again without remembering what we just did. I'm not so sure that's a good thing."

He grinned. "Okay, so next time we should try for the bedroom."

She patted his jeans, still bunched around his hips. "I think next time we should try to get all our clothes off. This makes me think we're still in high school."

"Is that so bad?"

She gave him a contented smile. "I guess not. Although I don't remember it being this good when I was in high school."

"I keep telling you. Knowing anatomy makes a difference."

As he spoke, he began to withdraw from her. He reached down to make sure the condom stayed in place. His gaze followed his actions and he saw the thin layer of protection was not covering him as it should have. A long tear had ripped it nearly in two, lengthwise.

"It broke," Nora said, her voice tight with horror and disbelief.

Stephen held in a groan. Damn. The potential consequences were obviously apparent to both of them. Even as his gut tightened, he told himself not to panic.

"It's all right," he said calmly. "Healthwise, I don't pose a risk to you. As for pregnancy—it's highly unlikely. It was just the one time."

"I know." The words sounded small. She slipped off the table and reached for her robe. "I'm sure everything is fine. It was just kind of unexpected."

"Agreed."

He disposed of the condom and couldn't help remembering what had happened when Courtney had realized that a difficult work schedule had made her forget to take her birth control pills. She'd been furious. Her anger had only increased when she'd found out she was pregnant. He'd been thrilled, but Courtney had thought the child would be inconvenient. Her new fellowship didn't leave time for motherhood.

As he fastened his jeans, he remembered their arguments. Courtney had wanted an abortion, but he'd begged her to keep the baby. Because selfishly he'd wanted a child. In the end, she'd given in and by doing so, she'd died. It was all his fault. He saw that now. But it was too late for him to change the past.

He couldn't go through that again, he told himself. Not an unplanned pregnancy or a reluctant mother-to-be. So Nora simply couldn't be pregnant.

He turned to face her. She stood by the counter, her robe covering her body, her hands shoved into her pockets, her shoulders hunched.

"Where are you in your cycle?" he asked.

"I'm really close to getting my period. If we had to have an accident, this is a really safe time." She raised her head and looked at him. "Look, Stephen, it's late and this has sort of put a damper on the evening. Why don't you head on home and we'll talk later?''

Part of him wanted to protest. He'd thought he would spend the night, holding her in his arms as they slept. But she was right about the mood-breaker. He was more than ready to get back to his own place.

''Are you sure you're all right?'' he asked.

''I'm fine. I wanted you to come over tonight. I'm not sorry about any of it. Okay?''

He walked over to her and kissed her mouth. ''I meant what I said before. You're special to me and I hope we can make this work.''

''Me, too.''

It took nearly fifteen more minutes, but Nora finally managed to hustle Stephen out of her house. What was it about men? When you wanted them to stay they couldn't wait to leave, and when you wanted to be alone, they clung like burrs.

When she was alone, she leaned against the front door and bit back a scream. Special. He thought she was special. She didn't know if she should laugh or cry. How special could she be when compared to his oh-so-perfect wife?

''What a night,'' she muttered as she turned off the living room lights and headed for her bedroom.

The sex had been amazing. She was willing to admit that she'd never experienced anything even close to that in her entire life. But in the future she could do without the confessions and mishaps. She hated knowing about his past, even though it made no sense that it would bother her. Why should she care that he was a widower?

She crossed to her bed and straightened the covers.

The scent of their lovemaking clung to the sheets. But she was too tired to change the linens tonight. Maybe in the morning.

Stephen married. And he'd nearly had a child. She didn't know what it all meant. So instead of trying to figure it out, she plopped onto the mattress and pulled open the top drawer of her nightstand. In the corner was a small notebook. She flipped open the pages and checked the last date, then added. When she'd finished, she closed the small book and pressed it to her chest.

She'd lied. Plain and simple. This wasn't a safe time for her at all. She was in the exact middle of her very regular cycle. She doubted even a rabbit would be more fertile than she was that night.

She didn't allow herself to think about the miracle of a baby. Instead she told herself that it was only one time and ignore the gleeful voice that whispered one time was all it took.

Chapter Nine

Nora was elbow-deep in a perm when the flowers arrived the next morning. Her senses went on alert the second the young man from the Canyon Florist walked into her shop. Saturday mornings were always busy and she had every single customer's attention as she paused long enough to sign the clipboard and collect the oversize vase. Normally loud conversation stilled and heads turned while she carefully pocketed the card and made room for the arrangement on the main reception counter.

"Flowers?" Mrs. Arnold said archly. "I wonder who they're from."

Nora gave the room a bright smile. "Aren't they beautiful?" She made a show of inhaling the sweet-spicy fragrance of the spring bouquet.

Jill was making an appointment with a customer. She glanced up at Nora, her expression knowing.

"They're lovely. I recognize the irises. What are those pink flowers?"

"Stargazer lilies," Nora told her. "The long stalks with the fluffy white blooms are English garden stock. What a perfect way to start my day." She gave another glowing smile and returned to her customer. "Now, what were you telling me about your grandson's new girlfriend?"

It took a little doing but in a matter of minutes, she'd managed to get the attention off herself and the opulent display scenting the room. Unfortunately with each new customer arrival, the flowers were commented upon. But Nora never offered the name of her benefactor and no one came out and asked. But they wondered and speculated and it made her crazy to be the subject of gossip. She'd already had enough of that to last a lifetime.

To make matters worse, she was trying to forget Stephen and their close encounter the previous night. The lingering contentment in her body and the beautiful flowers were a constant reminder of all that had happened between them…including the issues of his late wife and the broken condom. Other women could probably have adult affairs without so much as a ripple in the pond of their life. But not her. One night of incredible sex and her entire world was upside down.

A little after one that afternoon, Nora finally had a break in her schedule. She ducked into the small powder room at the rear of the shop and opened the card.
Thanks for last night.

She read it twice, then blinked and read it again. Thanks for last night? He had to be kidding. If he thought for a second that not signing his name was being subtle, he was crazy. Everyone was going to know everything, no thanks to him. What on earth was she going to do with him?

She glanced at her reflection in the oval mirror over the sink and smoothed back a strand of hair that had come loose from her French braid. Her makeup was still relatively fresh. She touched up her lipstick, then ducked out of the powder room and left the shop by the rear entrance. Her next appointment wasn't until one-thirty, which gave her plenty of time to give Stephen Remington a piece of her mind.

By circling around to the end of the block and using the rear entrance of the medical office, she managed to make her way into the business across the street from her shop without being seen by anyone. She found Nurse Rosie at the front counter, notating a chart.

"I need to see him," Nora said, barely able to look at the other woman. She felt as if everyone in town knew what they'd been doing the previous night.

"Is something wrong? His office hours are closed for the day, but if it's an emergency, he's still here."

Nora gritted her teeth. "No. It's personal. Just tell him that I need to see him."

What she wanted to do was force her way into his office and give in to the frustration flooding her. But that would only create more talk, which was exactly what she wanted to avoid.

Rosie studied her for a second before nodding and retreating to the rear of the building. The nurse returned in less than a minute and motioned for Nora to follow her. Nora thanked the other woman, stepped past her and into a large, paneled office, slammed the door behind her and gave into her temper.

"What is wrong with you?" she demanded, striding toward the desk and glaring at Stephen. "I don't want to think you did this on purpose, but despite my other reservations about you I've never thought you were completely stupid."

"How flattering," he said dryly, leaning back in his large leather chair. He didn't look upset, confused or even surprised at her invasion. If anything, he appeared faintly amused, which really annoyed her.

"Oh, sure. It's funny to you, because none of this matters. But I have a life here, damn you. Stop messing with it."

He rose to his feet. He was tall and lean and now she knew what he looked like naked. The slacks, shirt and tie made him look professional and appealing, but she was suddenly reminded that without his clothes, he was temptation incarnate. She had felt things with this man that she had never felt in her life. He'd made her respond in ways she hadn't thought possible, and even through her temper all she wanted was for him to grab her and start making love with her right there on his oversize desk.

He came around the desk, stopping when he was in front of her. After settling one hip on the wood surface, he folded his arms and gave her a patient smile.

"Want to tell me what has you all hot and bothered?"

She reached into her pants pocket and pulled out the card he'd had delivered along with the bouquet. Anger and frustration filled her until she wanted to throw something to relieve the tension. Instead all she could do was speak through gritted teeth. "You sent flowers and a note."

He took the envelope and pulled out the small card. "I don't understand. I thought last night was very special. I enjoyed myself, which is a feeling I think you share. The flowers were a way to say thank you, I'm thinking about you. It's just good manners."

"Good manners? What do they have to do with anything? We're talking about my *life*." She planted her hands on her hips and leaned toward him. "They're flowers, Stephen. Lord knows who saw your car parked in front of my house until all hours. Then you send flowers and a card thanking me for last night. I suppose taking an ad out in the local newspaper would have made it a little easier for people to figure out what's going on, but you certainly are not making it difficult by doing this."

She grabbed the card and envelope back from him and stuffed both back into her pocket. "I wanted this to be private," she reminded him. "Wasn't that our deal?"

He looked at her. Several emotions skittered across his hazel eyes, but she didn't know him well enough to read them. Then he reached toward her and brushed his fingertips against her cheek.

"You're right," he said simply. "I'm sorry. I wasn't thinking. All I knew was that I'd really enjoyed being with you and I wanted you to know." He dropped his hand to his side.

She opened her mouth, then closed it. "You're apologizing?"

"Yes. Of course. I was in the wrong. I knew you wanted to keep things quiet. You're not interested in gossip and neither am I. Lone Star Canyon is a small town. By sending flowers and a note like that, I've made us the object of interest and speculation. It was stupid. I wasn't thinking. I'm sorry.''

Her anger faded away as if it had never been. She couldn't ever remember a man apologizing to her before—not with such ease and sincerity. ''Thank you,'' she said. ''I accept your apology.''

His hazel eyes stared at her steadily. ''Do you believe me?''

She bit her lower lip, then nodded. ''Yes. I do.''

He stood, reached for her waist, leaned against the desk and pulled her up against him. Her belly pressed against the apex of his thighs and her hands instinctively came up around his shoulders.

''Good,'' he said with a pleased grin. ''So how about a rematch?''

Before she could answer, his mouth was on hers.

She told herself to be furious. That he was being an insensitive clod. That she should pull back, slap him, then give him a large piece of her mind. But his mouth felt too good against her own. In a single night he'd figured out how much she enjoyed his deep, lingering, sensual kisses and now he was using her own weakness against herself.

''I want you,'' he breathed, trailing his mouth against her cheek and down her throat. ''You make me crazy and I can't get enough of you. Tell me when I can see you again.''

She pushed against his shoulders, but the gesture was halfhearted at best. ''Someone could walk in and see us.''

''Let 'em get their own girl.''

Despite her need to stay in control and resist him, she couldn't help laughing. ''You're so difficult.''

''I'm so good. You want me, too. I can tell.''

He looked at her and she knew there was plenty of passion to read in her expression. She *did* want him, even though she shouldn't.

She finally found the strength to free herself. "I have to get back to the shop. I have a one-thirty appointment."

He touched her swollen mouth. "Soon?" he asked.

She wanted to say no. She wanted to say that their single night had been a mistake. She wanted to remind him that the second condom had broken and that could create its own kind of trouble. But she didn't say anything. Instead she took the coward's way out and simply ran from his office without once looking back.

"Go out with me."

Stephen's voice was low and insistent, and made Nora want to purr. She leaned back in the receptionist's chair and resisted the need to turn so that she could see out the front window of her shop. Stephen was just across the street...close enough that they could be in each other's arms in less than three minutes. The idea was tempting.

"I can't," she said, hoping her resolve would hold out through the entire phone conversation. If he kept after her for too long, she knew she would weaken. Already she could feel her body beginning to tremble at the thought of being with him. She longed to see him, to talk with him, and most of all, to make love with him.

"It's been nearly a week," he reminded her. "You're avoiding me. What I want to know is why?"

She swallowed her guilt. "*Avoiding* is a strong term. I've been busy. Because I was out sick for so long, I had a lot of catching up to do. Now that's taken care of and I'm tired.''

"I want to believe you," he said, "but I'm not sure that I do."

She winced but he had every right to his reservations. The truth was she *had* been avoiding him and she intended to continue doing so for as long as possible. If she were to explain that, he would ask her why and that's where her argument stalled. She didn't have a good reason...except for the voice whispering in her head. It told her that seeing him again would be very dangerous, even though it didn't tell her why.

Nora had her own reasons as well. She was still getting used to the fact that Stephen had been happily married up until the death of his wife. What if he was still in love with the woman? That was too awful to think about—being with him then would be too much like being with a married man. Something she would never do.

And even if he was starting to get over his loss, she wasn't willing to be put in a position where she would constantly be compared to someone else. How was she supposed to measure up to Courtney Remington, pediatric neurosurgeon?

"What's the real reason?" he asked. "What don't you want me to know?"

"There isn't any deep, dark secret." That was only a small lie, she told herself. Her concerns were private, not secret. "I enjoyed our night together, but I don't feel compelled to repeat it."

"Why not? I know you had a good time. Didn't you like all the things I did to you?"

She sighed and swung back and forth in the chair. Yes, she'd liked them very much. Even now, just thinking about them was enough to make her insides get all squishy. "It's more complicated than that."

He lowered his voice. "No. It's very simple. I want to undress you, then kiss you until you can't catch your breath. I want to nibble that ticklish spot just behind your knees and lick my way up your thighs. I want to make you tense and scream and fly, then I want to be inside of you and do it all again."

He painted a very vivid picture with just a few words, she thought as her throat tightened and it became more difficult to breathe. "Yes, well, that would be nice, but then what? We have nothing in common."

He chuckled. "What about the physical attraction?"

"That's just chemistry."

"Hey, don't dismiss my favorite subject in school. Besides, we have plenty to talk about, Nora. You know that as well as I do. I think what's troubling you the most isn't that we may or may not have enough to say to each other, it's how good things are when we're too busy doing other things. I think you're scared."

Full points to the opposition, she thought, not sure how to answer him. "I can't explain it any better than I have. This isn't something I can do right now." She swallowed. "I have to go, Stephen. Goodbye."

She hung up without waiting for him to respond. For a few minutes she just sat in the chair, wondering if he would accept her decision or if he would cross the street and pound on her door, insisting that she speak with him.

A couple of minutes went by and there was only silence. Obviously, he'd accepted her view of things and was going to let it all go. A part of her was disappointed that he hadn't been willing to try harder, but for the most part, she was pleased. Life would be easier without him around to make things complicated.

She leaned back in her chair and looked at the shop. It was after seven on Thursday and everyone else had gone home. The scents of the shampoo, perm solution and hair spray lingered in the room. She'd worked hard to buy the Snip 'n Clip salon and now every bit of it was hers. She had a thriving business, a small nest egg and—she touched her stomach—the possibility of a baby on the way.

Nora smiled to herself as she pressed against her flat belly. Was she pregnant? It was probably too soon to tell, but she couldn't help hoping that she was. She'd always wanted children, and as there wasn't any Mr. Right in her future, this might be her only chance. If Stephen wasn't interested in a long-term romantic relationship with a woman, he was unlikely to want to be involved with a child. Which meant she wouldn't have to worry about him hanging around wanting to play dad. The baby could be hers alone.

She held on to the promise of that glorious future. She knew that she could be a good mother—she'd had a wonderful role model. Her child would grow up with plenty of love and support, just as she had.

"Please God," she whispered into the night. "Let me be pregnant."

Just a few more days, she told herself. Then she could take the test and find out for sure.

Myrna Nelson was as frail as a crane, all long skinny legs and hollow bones. She walked into Ste-

phen's office with a deliberate slowness that set off
alarm bells. He motioned her into one of the chairs
in front of his desk, but instead of going around and
settling into his leather seat, he sat next to her and
took her too-thin hand in his.

"I have to tell you, Myrna, you're fading away,"
he said, staring deeply into her light blue eyes.
"You've lost three more pounds in the past month.
You're too thin. Why aren't you eating?"

She gave a delicate shrug that emphasized the boni-
ness of her shoulders. Myrna had never been a large
woman, but until her recent bout with cancer, she'd
been vibrant. She'd been active in her church, an avid
gardener and was known for preparing a secret recipe
of brownies so wonderful that she'd had dozens of
marriage proposals in the four years of her widow-
hood.

In the past few months, all that had changed. Her
surgery had been a success, her radiation was over
and her prognosis was excellent. She was seventy-
four, but until recently she'd had the energy and joy
of life of a woman still in her thirties.

"Tell me what's wrong," he insisted.

"Nothing. I'm fine. A little tired." She gave a sigh
then smiled. "You're kind to worry."

"Are you going to church services? Working in
your garden?"

She shook her head. "It all seems like so much
trouble."

He studied her more closely. Previously, she'd always worn bright colors. Today her shapeless dress
was dark and wrinkled. Her mouth was pale, which
made him remember that until the cancer, he'd never
seen her without makeup. Now she never wore it. Her

hair was clean but unstyled, her nails were uneven. She was a woman who didn't care about much anymore.

"Don't let apathy do what the cancer couldn't," he said. "I'm not ready to lose you."

She gave him a faint smile that didn't reach her eyes. "Thank you, Dr. Remington. I'll be fine."

She rose slowly and collected her purse, then shuffled out of the room. He followed her, wishing he had a magic answer. Myrna Nelson had lost her reason to live. Something about her illness had made her sink into hopelessness.

As he held open the front door for her, he automatically glanced across the street. The bright afternoon light reflected off the windows of Nora's shop, so he couldn't see inside, but he imagined the beautiful woman working there.

As he watched, one of her clients stepped onto the street. She was about the same age as Mrs. Nelson, but unlike Myrna, this woman had a spring in her step. She paused to admire her reflection in the shop window, patting her hair as she gave herself a satisfied smile.

Stephen stared at her for a moment as an idea was born. "I want to see you in two weeks," he told his patient.

"Whatever you say," she murmured as she shuffled toward her car.

In the meantime he was going to try a little unconventional therapy, and he knew just the person to assist him. Assuming he could get Nora to agree.

He waited until Myrna had driven away before crossing the street and walking toward the Snip 'n Clip. While he told himself he was doing this all for a patient, he knew in his heart he'd been looking for an excuse to see Nora. She'd been avoiding him for nearly a week and she'd neatly shut him down on the phone the previous evening. What he didn't know was why. What had happened to make her change her mind about him? Had he done something wrong or was she getting cold feet? Not that there was anything cold about her. She was the most sensual, passionate woman he'd ever known. Just thinking about being with her and touching her was enough to get his blood bubbling.

He paused outside her shop so he could calm his thoughts. He didn't want to walk into the all-female enclave while obviously aroused.

So instead of focusing on Nora's body, he thought about her mind. Her quick wit and biting tongue didn't scare him—instead she made him laugh. Being with her was different from being with Courtney. With Nora, he felt comfortable, as if he didn't have to keep proving himself. He hated to think ill of his late wife, but Courtney had always been pushing him. She'd had dreams and goals, and she hadn't been shy about making sure he was aware of them and moving in the right direction.

The glass door of the shop opened and Nora stuck out her head. ''Are you going to stand there forever, or did you want to come in?''

She was gorgeous, he thought, taking in the long-sleeved white shirt tucked into red jeans. Her hair was loose and curly, tumbling over her shoulders in a way that made him want to run his fingers through the curls and bury his face in the softness.

''Stephen?''

''What? Oh.'' She was still looking at him. He realized that while he couldn't see in the shop, everyone there could see out. "Sorry. I was thinking."

"We could tell. Did you want something?"

"Yes. I want to talk to you. About a patient of mine. I need your help."

She sighed heavily, then pushed the door open wider. "You might as well come in, then. You've already created a stir."

"Ever gracious," he murmured as he followed her into the feminine world of Nora's salon.

As soon as he stepped into the waiting area, he was assaulted by too many smells. Chemicals and perfumes, some pleasant, some strong enough to make him want to cough, filled the air. Everyone but himself was female, most sitting in large chairs and covered with multicolored plastic capes. He saw women with tight rollers in their hair, women adorned with bits of foil that made them look as if they were trying to contact alien life-forms. Someone was getting her nails done, while another was being teased and sprayed to within an inch of her life. And every single person in the place was staring at him.

He gave a wave. "Good afternoon, ladies. Don't mind me. I'm here to talk to Nora."

"So we guessed," an older woman in curlers said with a smirk. "So, Nora. A doctor. Your mother will be so proud."

Nora looked at him and raised her eyebrows as if to say, "I told you so." Then she pointed to the rear of the salon. "My office is back here."

He followed her past deep bowls with reclining chairs and several dryers anchored to the wall. If this was a world of beauty, he didn't want to visit again.

The walls were too pink and everything about the place screamed that he didn't belong.

She waited for him to step into her office, then closed the door behind him. He glanced around. At least here the walls were cream and there wasn't a single floral print or flounce in sight. Instead, a worn desk filled the small space. There was a four-drawer file cabinet and fax machine tucked on a small table in the corner.

Nora planted her bottom on the desk and stared at him. "So what do you want?"

"You."

It hadn't been what he'd meant to say, but once the word was out, he couldn't call it back. He stepped closer and drew her to him. She didn't protest, not even when he kissed her. She tasted sweet and willing and soon they were locked in a passionate embrace.

"Why are you avoiding me?" he asked as her body surged against him. The soft pressure of her breasts was pure torture.

"I'm not."

"Liar. Either you hated what we did together, or you're scared. Which is it?"

The challenge got the expected response. She straightened and glared at him. "I'm not frightened of you or any man."

"Uh-huh. So the sex was lousy?"

She looked past his shoulder. "No. It was very nice."

"So you're scared."

She returned her attention to him, trying to slay him with a glare. "There is a third alternative."

"Tell me what it is."

She opened her mouth, then closed it. Fire flared

from her big brown eyes, but it had nothing to do with passion and everything to do with frustration.

Triumph filled him. "Face it. You want me, but you're scared. So you're avoiding me. I understand." He leaned close. "Coward."

She hissed, but didn't speak.

He laughed and cupped her face. "I adore being with you."

Her expression tightened. "Be careful. I might get a swelled head and think you actually want a relationship with me."

That got his attention. He dropped his hands to his sides. "Have you changed your mind about keeping things simple between us? Is that why you've been avoiding me?"

"Oh, isn't that just like a man. There you go, assuming if the sex was halfway decent I must be picking out china and planning a wedding. Amazingly enough, Dr. Stephen Remington, I have no interest in you that way." She pressed her hands to her chest. "Oh, no. Something that isn't actually about you. How will you survive?"

Her belittling attack made him feel better. "Do you want to hear why I needed to see you or what?"

"Avoiding an ugly truth. Also, how like a man. Yes, tell me what's wrong."

He sat on the desk and patted the space next to him. When she'd joined him, he explained about Myrna and his theory that she'd lost interest in life.

"I see the women coming out of your shop all the time," he said. "They feel vital and attractive. I would like you to pay Myrna a house call. I think some attention would go a long way to making her feel better. I'll take care of the bill."

She'd been smiling at him right up until he mentioned money. "I don't need your financial assistance. I'll do this for Myrna because I've always liked her. In fact, she was my Sunday School teacher for about four years, so I owe her. I'll head over first thing in the morning."

"I want to go with you."

She shrugged. "Suit yourself. Watching someone get a shampoo and set can be pretty boring."

"Not when you're in the room. I'd pay just to watch you sleep." He leaned close. "Naked, of course."

Color stained her cheeks. "Of course."

"So when can I see you again?"

She sighed heavily. "I'm never getting rid of you, am I?"

"Not in this lifetime."

"So I should just give in?"

"Absolutely." He leaned close and nibbled on her earlobe. "I promise to make you faint with pleasure. You want to come to my place this time?"

She shivered. "F-fine. What time?"

"Seven," he said with a straight face, not letting her know for a second that he'd heard the tremor of desire in her voice.

Chapter Ten

Nora arrived promptly at six-fifty-nine, then paced by her car until exactly seven. She couldn't believe she'd agreed to this. It was insane. It was crazy, and so was she.

She looked at the single-story garden apartment complex. The units were relatively new. She wondered why he hadn't bought a house rather than renting. Was it because he was new in town and hadn't had time, or was his stay in Lone Star Canyon temporary? Not that she cared. If Stephen Remington left town tomorrow, she would be a happy camper.

Nora sucked in a breath and reminded herself that it was never a good policy to lie to anyone, especially one's self. Of course she cared if Stephen stayed or went. Maybe she didn't care a whole lot, but she had some interest in the man. After all, she was here to make love with him.

Her stomach quivered in anticipation. She pressed
a hand against her belly to try to quiet her nerves.
What was there to worry about? She'd been with the
man before and everything had worked out well. She
found herself melting whenever he got within touching distance. Obviously their bodies connected on a
very basic level. They were both adults, and neither
of them wanted a long-term, emotional commitment.
What was not to like?

She squared her shoulders and headed toward his
front door. Everything was fine, she told herself, but
she didn't believe that, either. Nothing felt right about
this. Although she was looking forward to seeing Stephen, she found herself uncomfortable with the
thought of being intimate with him again. Which was
crazy. The man made her incredibly hot. If he'd
pushed her even a little, they would have done it earlier that afternoon, right in her office. So why was
this different?

She didn't have any answers when she knocked on
his front door. He opened it instantly and smiled at
her.

"I thought maybe you'd chicken out," he said with
a glinting smile.

He wore jeans and a long-sleeved shirt. He'd obviously showered—his hair was still damp and his
feet were bare. His jaw looked freshly shaved. He was
a good-looking man. Intelligent, compassionate and
darned good in bed. Just to make things interesting,
he wanted her as his lover. It was a pretty lethal combination. She had to swallow against the sudden knot
in her throat, and the quivering in her stomach increased to a steady throb.

"I don't scare so easy," she told him.

"I know. It's part of your charm." He motioned for her to enter the apartment.

She stepped inside, taking in the large living room with an eating alcove and a kitchen to the left. On the right was a hallway. The apartment was spacious, with big windows and hardwood floors. But as she looked around, taking in the plain but functional furniture and the complete absence of any personal items on either the walls or the tables, she had the strongest urge to introduce color and personality to the room.

The walls and blinds were cream, the sofa and chairs a blue-beige plaid, the wood, light oak. There wasn't a scrap of color or plant life in sight.

"Are you afraid someone will think you actually live here?" she asked as she took a seat on the sofa. The cushions were plump and comfortable, but she couldn't help thinking she was in a furniture showroom rather than someone's home.

"What do you mean?" he asked as he followed her into the room. "You don't like my decorating choices?"

"I don't know. You haven't made any. What about artwork or pictures, or even a plant or two? The room cries out for color."

He frowned. "I didn't think of that. When I moved from Boston I sold everything I had and started fresh. You think I need color?"

"Something. Even hotel rooms have pictures on the walls."

He glanced around as if seeing the place for the first time. "Maybe you're right." He shrugged off the conversation and turned toward the kitchen. "Want something to drink? I have both white and red wine."

"I'm a little tired," she said, telling herself it

wasn't exactly a lie. "I'm afraid alcohol will put me on my butt, so I'd rather have a diet soda if you have one. Or water."

"One diet soda on ice, coming up," he said easily, and stepped into the kitchen.

Nora breathed a sigh of relief. At least he hadn't questioned her refusal of the wine. She'd wondered if he would guess her real reason for avoiding it— namely that until she was sure she wasn't pregnant, she wasn't going to touch alcohol.

Stephen returned with two glasses. He set them on the coffee table, then sat next to her. Much to her dismay, he was close enough to set her body on fire. She felt both aroused and jumpy, neither of which was helped by him putting his hand on her knee.

"We have to talk," he said, his expression serious.

She didn't want to talk, but she couldn't tell him that. He would think she wanted to get right to the sex and she wasn't sure if she could do that tonight. Nothing felt right—her skin was prickly, as if it was too tight, and her heart was all fluttery and her head kind of hurt but kind of didn't.

She leaned forward and picked up her drink, mostly so she didn't have to look at him. "Say what you'd like. I'm listening."

"I was hoping the communication thing would go two ways."

"Why?"

He laughed. "Because it generally makes things easier. I say something, you respond, then you say something."

"Okay. Say something."

He shifted on the sofa, then she felt his hand on her back. His touch was light and warm and made her want to snuggle closer to him. Which was darned annoying.

"You seem nervous," he said. "Did I coerce you into coming over tonight? Would you like to leave?"

She took a sip of her soda, then put the glass back on the table. Which, unfortunately, wasn't enough time for her to gather her thoughts together. "I don't feel that you forced me to come here. I'll admit to being a little nervous. The entire situation is strange. I guess part of it is that while in theory I agree with your concept about adults having a sexually monogamous, commitment-free relationship, the practice isn't that simple."

Which was as close to the truth as she was willing to get. There was no way she was going to tell him that she was distracted by the idea of being pregnant and the nagging belief that if they continued to be lovers that her feelings for him might go in a direction neither of them wanted.

"I understand," he said. "Obviously I'm such a good lover that you're completely overwhelmed. I understand. It's been a real problem for me all my life. Women experience such bliss in my arms that they feel compelled to worship me and service me with slavish devotion. It's pretty embarrassing."

She sprang to her feet and spun to face him. Laughter danced in his eyes but his expression was completely serious. She raised her eyebrows and glared down at him.

"I'm wearing sandals," she said, lifting a foot to prove the fact. "So I'm not dressed to wade through all the manure you're shoveling."

He collapsed back in mock shock. "You don't feel

compelled to worship me? To spend your life adoring the very ground on which I walk?''

''Not even close.''

He pushed their drinks to the far side of the coffee table, then patted the wooden surface in front of him. Reluctantly Nora sat where he'd indicated. Now they were facing each other and as close as they'd been before. Which was not a good idea. Especially when Stephen took her hands in his and stared deeply into her eyes.

''Are you uncomfortable because you're concerned that everyone in town will figure out we're seeing each other? I know you're sensitive to being the object of speculation.''

He was being intuitive and kind. A lethal combination, because it was so rare in a man. ''That's some of it. Eventually everyone knows everyone else's business.''

His fingers were warm as they rubbed against hers. He squeezed. ''And I didn't help that when I sent the flowers last Saturday. I'm sorry.''

''You've already apologized. It's fine. No one read the card but me.'' And he would never know that she'd tucked it away in a small box at the back of her closet with all the other special mementos of her life.

He glanced down, then back at her. ''At the risk of starting trouble, does any of your reluctance come from the fact that I was married before? You seemed surprised to find out I was a widower.''

Nora felt as if he'd suddenly ripped open her protective cover and could see down into the darkness of her soul. She felt small and inadequate, but when she tried to pull her hands free of his, he wouldn't let her.

"I guess," she mumbled, not looking at him. "Not really, but in a way."

"You want to explain that?"

"No."

"Nora." He didn't say anything else, just waited until she finally raised her head and met his gaze. "Courtney doesn't have anything to do with you and me."

"Yes, she does. She's still a part of your life. You're in love with her, which makes me feel like I'm helping you cheat or something. I'm not the kind of woman who gets involved with married men."

"I never thought you were. But I'm not married. Courtney has been gone for a long time. You're right about my feelings for her. I'll always love her, but why would that affect us?"

She shrugged rather than try to explain something that didn't make sense to herself. She didn't want him to still be in love with his dead wife. Maybe that wasn't fair or made her a petty, shallow person. Either way, she was uncomfortable with the situation.

"I don't want you thinking about her when you're with me and I can't tell if you're doing that or not."

She'd spoken without thinking, the words coming in a rush. Once they were said, she wanted to call them back. But she couldn't. All she could do was press her lips together and hope he changed the subject.

She hoped in vain.

He dropped her hands and reached up to cup her face. A slow smile tugged at his lips. "Nora, you're a force of nature. It's physically impossible to think

of anyone else while I'm with you. I'm not just talking about making love, either. Just having a conversation requires me to focus all my attention on you.
If I don't, you'll grind me into dust. You're beautiful,
bright and funny, but you're never, ever easy.''

Some of her concern eased. ''You think?''

''Absolutely. You don't scare me, but you do get
my attention.''

She wanted to believe him. She wanted to know
that his past was firmly behind him and wouldn't have
anything to do with his present. But he hadn't said he
wasn't in love with Courtney anymore and that was
really what Nora wanted to hear. Not that she would
ever tell him that. It violated the rules of noninvolve-
ment.

He leaned forward and brushed her mouth with his.
''Are we all right?'' he asked.

She nodded. She knew that he was really asking if
they could make love now. Her entire body heated
with anticipation. She wanted to be with him, touching him, being touched by him. But more than that,
she wanted him to hold her close and promise that
everything would be all right. The sexual desire she
could accept—the need for comfort terrified her. She
didn't want to be vulnerable to a man, not ever again.

So she pulled back, then rose to her feet. ''I can't,''
she said, backing away from him.

''What's wrong?''

''Nothing specific. I just think we need to put
things on hold for a while.''

He stood as well, but didn't approach her.
'' 'Things' as in our relationship?''

''Yes. I can't make love with you tonight.''

She waited for the anger, the accusation, but Stephen was quiet. He studied her, then nodded. "Are you going to tell me why?"

Because she was hurting inside and she didn't know why. Because she was confused and afraid and somehow he'd managed to twist her world around until she didn't recognize it anymore.

"No," she said curtly. "I'm going to tell you that I'm not willing to have sex with you right now. You can't order me into your bed. We don't vote, this isn't a democracy. If I'm not willing, then it doesn't happen. And I'm not."

She raised her chin slightly, prepared to take him on. But there wasn't a fight. Only silence. Stephen stared at a point just past her left shoulder. She could hear the faint ticking of a clock in the kitchen. Somewhere outside a car engine started. Finally he looked at her.

"Are you still going to help me with Mrs. Nelson tomorrow?"

It was not the question she'd expected. "Of course. Why would that change?"

He gave her a humorless smile. "The rules around here seem to be written in quicksand. I was just checking." His gaze sharpened. "Did you get your period yet?"

"No. I'm not due for a few more days."

She'd spoken without thinking, because he'd caught her off guard. As soon as the words were out, Nora closed her eyes and groaned. Not only was Stephen capable of adding, he was a doctor so he knew what the numbers meant.

She risked a quick glance and saw comprehension dawning. He nodded slightly.

"It wasn't a safe time last week."

He wasn't asking a question, but she went ahead and answered it all the same. "Not really." She swallowed. "But it was just the one time and the odds of anything happening are really slim, don't you think? I mean nonexistent. Statistically, we're fine."

He shoved his hands into his jeans front pockets. "I want you to take a pregnancy test tomorrow. Then we'll know for sure."

She took a step back. "No. That's not necessary. It doesn't matter if I'm pregnant. I mean, it won't matter to you. You don't want a relationship with a woman so you certainly don't want to worry about being a father. Which is fine. If I am pregnant, which I'm not, but if I am, I'll handle it all myself. I love kids. I've always wanted them and my work is such that I can be flexible with my hours. No one has to know you're the father. I'd sign whatever you like, so you wouldn't have to worry about me coming after you for money or anything. Really. It would be no big deal."

His expression had tightened as she spoke until it was as if he wore a cold, unreadable mask. Nora took another step back and found herself pressed up against the fireplace.

"I realize that we don't know each other very well," he said in a slow, angry voice. "So let me explain a few things to you. First of all, I take my responsibilities very seriously. I am not the kind of man who would walk away from his child and I resent the implication that you could buy me off by promising to never come after any financial support."

"I didn't mean that in a bad way," she said hastily. "I only meant—"

His glare cut her off in midsentence. "You should

have told me the truth that night. If you're pregnant, we'll deal with it together.''

''But I don't want you involved.''

''Too bad. It's my baby, too, and I *will* be involved, so get used to that.''

''But you don't want children.''

Some of the hardness left his face. ''Actually, I do.''

She didn't know what to say to that. Stephen was interested in being a father? Was that possible? She'd been afraid if he found out about the pregnancy that he would want her to get rid of the life growing inside of her. She'd never considered he would want to be a part of its life.

''If you're pregnant,'' he said, ''I will be the father, I will act like the father and I will be a part of my child's life. If you're pregnant, we're getting married.''

Nora didn't remember leaving Stephen's apartment. One minute she'd been standing there listening to him say that if she was pregnant, he expected them to get married, and the next thing she knew, she'd pulled into her own driveway and was running into the house.

She fumbled with the lock on the front door, then threw herself inside and staggered to the sofa. She collapsed onto the familiar, soft cushions, pulling her legs to her chest and hugging herself as if she had to hold in incredible pain. Her body ached, she was fighting tears and nothing in her world made sense anymore. What was going on?

She huddled in the darkness searching for answers, but she didn't even understand the questions. Worse, she didn't know what was upsetting her the most. Was it his pronouncement, or something more frightening? She had a bad feeling that what rattled her the most was that Stephen had been able to figure out what she'd been thinking. He'd looked at her strange behavior, obviously wanting to be with him yet resisting the intimacy, and had quickly figured out her greatest concerns. First, that she wasn't comfortable about his feelings for his late wife, and second, that she might be pregnant.

No one—certainly not a man—had ever understood her so completely. How could he do that, and after they'd known each other for such a short period of time? She hated that he could read her mind.

She pushed herself into a sitting position. "I won't marry him," she announced to the darkness. "He can't make me."

Married? Her? To him? It was too strange to consider. But what if she was pregnant? Did he really want to be a part of his child's life?

She told herself she hated the idea of sharing her child with anyone, but the feeling wasn't all that forceful. She liked Stephen most of the time. Maybe sharing the burden would be kind of nice. Although getting married was out of the question. If there was a baby, they could discuss co-parenting or something equally civilized.

That decided, some of her equilibrium returned. She turned on the lamp by the sofa, then walked into the kitchen. She'd collected her mail earlier but hadn't looked through it in her rush to get ready to go over to Stephen's. Now she absently flipped through the stack of catalogs and envelopes. Her fingers fumbled when she came across a thick, creamy envelope. The printed return address was the Darby ranch.

Cold seeped through Nora. She stiffened in anticipation, but that didn't stop a stab of pain when she opened the envelope and saw a wedding invitation. She pulled out the elegant stationery.

Because we love each other...

She brushed her index finger across the first line, feeling the ridges of the embossed printing. Jack and Katie's names were below, the letters entwined, joining much as their lives would join when they married.

Because we love each other. The words repeated themselves over and over until they filled the room. Jack and Katie were in love. That's why they were getting married. They were going to face opposition from members of both families and years of talk in town. Katie's father might never forgive his daughter for what he would see as a betrayal. But none of that mattered to them. They had each other and they would face the world strengthened by their love.

She'd seen them together and with Katie's son, Shane. She'd felt their affection, their commitment. It glowed as brilliantly as the sun, and when she was too close to them, her skin felt as if it had been burned.

Tears trickled down her cheeks. She told herself she was being silly, that none of this mattered. But the words didn't help. The tears fell faster and faster, a physical symbol of the pain ripping her apart inside. No man had ever loved her the way Jack loved Katie. Her own father had walked out on all his children years before. David Fitzgerald had married someone else. She'd been on dozens of dates, but not one man had been able or willing to see past her prickly facade to the softhearted woman inside.

She was empty and lonely and no one knew. Not even Stephen, who would marry her if she carried his baby, but would only ever love Courtney.

She tried to tell herself she didn't care, not about him or any of it. She would go to her brother's wedding and wish him the best because she loved him. Because she believed that Katie and Shane were going to make him very happy. She would hold her head high and never let the world know how she was broken inside.

As she sank onto a kitchen chair she couldn't help wishing that Stephen was with her. That he would pull her close and hold her until all the tears were gone and she felt safe again. Which only made her cry harder because caring about him was worse than foolish. It was a steep, slick road to disappointment. He might like her and he might want her, but he would never love her. Not as long as he was in love with someone else.

Chapter Eleven

Stephen set his coffee mug on the worn table in front of him, then fingered the hand-crocheted place mat and lace-edged napkins. Myrna Nelson's small house was sparkling clean, tidy and filled with a measure of things handmade with obvious care and love. Even the sharp smell of nail polish couldn't overpower the scent of potpourri wafting from small dishes scattered throughout the kitchen and living room.

"I think you made the right choice," Nora was saying as she applied nail polish to the other woman's wrinkled and trembling hand. "Pink is always flattering."

Myrna raised her free hand and blew gently on her painted nails. "I've always liked it. Pink is such a happy color."

Although Stephen had requested Nora's presence at Myrna's house and had tagged along to watch the transformation, he'd stayed in the background during the visit. Nora had come prepared with a portable shampoo bowl, curlers and a complete manicure set. The small kitchen had been transformed into a palace of beauty and he could already see the difference in his patient.

The Myrna who had greeted them at the door had looked bent and tired. Now, with her white hair freshly washed and curled, she had a sparkle in her faded blue eyes. She smiled more and had even excused herself to put on lipstick. As she gazed at her pink-tipped nails, she seemed to sit a little straighter and speak a little louder.

Stephen had always respected the mind's ability to influence the body. Time after time in his Boston emergency room he'd seen patients survive awful traumas, and people who should have been fine pass away. The former were often in the center of a warm, loving family, with hopes and dreams, and plenty to live for, while many of the latter were alone and lonely. He was glad that Myrna was responding to Nora's ministrations. He didn't plan to lose his patient anytime soon.

Nora laughed at something the older woman had said. Stephen turned his attention to the beautiful brunette wearing a green short-sleeved dress. She'd pulled her hair back into a braid, but a few curls had loosened and brushed against her cheek. Her big brown eyes avoided his gaze and she seemed jumpy around him. Not surprising considering their conversation the previous night.

He might be having a child with this woman. The concept was difficult to grasp. But as he watched her care for Myrna, he knew that Nora was going to be the best kind of mother—patient, loving and supportive. Nothing like Courtney.

The disloyal thought made him uncomfortable, so he pushed it away. Instead he tried to figure out how he felt about the possibility of Nora being pregnant. He hadn't thought he would have another chance at a child. Part of him was terrified, yet he couldn't help being a little pleased, too. Still, a baby would change everything. Was he ready for that? Did he have a choice?

He meant what he'd told Nora. If she was pregnant, he would marry her. He wanted to be a part of his child's life from the moment he was sure of its existence until he breathed his last. At least she'd been adamant about having the baby. He realized they'd never discussed any other alternative. Which was something else that was different. Courtney had resisted carrying the baby to term. They'd argued dozens of times until he'd finally convinced her to keep their child. If it had been left up to his wife, she would have terminated her pregnancy.

Although he hated thinking ill of Courtney, he had to admit that despite being a doctor, she wasn't very compassionate. She never connected with her patients and was careful to keep a professional distance between herself and her patient's family. She might have intuitively understood why they were ill, but she never touched their hearts. Not Nora. The woman sitting in front of him jumped in emotionally with both feet. She was fearless with her heart—at least where the rest of the world was concerned. She didn't trust men easily.

"You know all about the feud, don't you, Dr. Remington?" Myrna asked.

Stephen forced himself to pay attention to the conversation. "Yes. I've heard bits and pieces and Nora has filled me in on some of the details."

"She has a unique perspective on both the families." Myrna leaned toward him and lowered her voice conspiratorially. "David Fitzgerald was a fool to let her go."

Stephen couldn't help glancing at Nora. She stiffened slightly, then gave a tiny shrug as if to say talk like this couldn't be helped. She finished with the second coat of nail polish and screwed the top into place. After blowing on Myrna's nails, she opened a bottle of clear liquid.

"David was a long time ago," she said calmly. "We were both too young to be thinking about getting married. We couldn't be sure we were making the correct choice."

Myrna raised her eyebrows. "You're right about that. David sure didn't. Fern is a weak-willed woman who only complains. Those girls of hers are a handful. David works long hours keeping the ranch going, getting no thanks from his father." She leaned toward Stephen. "Aaron, David's father, is a bit of a tyrant."

"So I've heard."

"Nora here—" she nodded at the woman sitting across from her "—would have sassed him right back. I think that's one of the reasons he didn't want his son marrying her. It takes the right kind of man to handle a strong, intelligent woman. My Bert knew exactly what to do with me and I suspect you, Dr. Remington, have the gift as well."

"No matchmaking on weekends," Stephen said firmly. "You need to save that sort of thing for midweek."

But Myrna wasn't going to be put off so easily. "I've seen how you look at her, Doctor. My eyesight might not be what it was, but I can still see a thing or two."

Stephen allowed his gaze to drift over Nora, who just a week ago had made him remember the complete joy of making love with a responsive woman. "Nora is practically a goddess. Mere mortal man can't help being tempted. But that doesn't mean he's allowed to touch."

Nora rolled her eyes. "A goddess? Can't you do better than that?"

"Not this early in the morning."

Myrna smiled. "You like that she sasses you."

"It's one of her best features."

Myrna patted Nora's hand. "See, dear. There's hope."

Nora gave him an insincere smile. "My heart is going pitty-pat at the thought of this handsome man worshipping at my feet. I swear I feel a swoon coming on."

She finished the manicure and began to pack up her supplies. Myrna reached for her purse, but Nora wouldn't let her pay a dime for the services. Stephen figured he would settle up with her later. In the meantime, his patient glowed with life and interest.

"Promise me you'll call one or two of your friends and have lunch with them," he said as he rose to his feet.

Myrna stood up and waved her still-damp nails in front of her. "I think that's a grand idea. I've been meaning to for the past month or so, but I haven't had the energy."   •

But she did now, he thought, pleased with the

change in her. Physically Myrna had been healed for a long time, but it had taken a little extra effort to mend her heart and spirit. He gave his patient a hug, careful to stay clear of her fresh manicure, then he picked up Nora's tote bag and headed for the car. Five minutes later they pulled out of Myrna's driveway.

"Thanks for doing that," he said as he turned onto the main highway leading back to town. "I had a feeling that Myrna needed a little attention to get her back among the living."

"I was happy to help. People think beauty shops are all about hair and nails, but there's a lot of psychology going on as well."

He glanced at her, taking in her elegant profile and the way she was careful not to look at him. "I'm sorry about the matchmaking back there."

"It's not your fault. Besides, I'm used to it by now. Once I turned twenty-five, most of the women in town considered it their sacred duty to get me married."

"Yet here you are, deliciously single."

She pressed her lips together. "I'm not sure of the appeal of marriage. The chitchat you heard at Myrna's is nothing compared with what I hear at the shop. I know the details of nearly every marriage in town. The good and the bad, and from what I've been told, there's a whole lot more of the bad."

"How much of that is because some marriages are in trouble and how much of it is because people tend to talk more about what's wrong in their lives than what's right?"

"I hadn't thought about that." She adjusted her seat belt. "But you're right. My clients rarely mention their relationships when things are going well."

He turned left in front of the medical office and

drove around to the rear parking lot. Once there, he turned off the engine but didn't step out of the car.

The sweet scent of her body drifted to him. He wanted to reach out and touch the loose curls around her face, then pull her to him so he could kiss her. He wanted to slide his hands over her body, holding her close, making her want him as much as he wanted her.

Nora was unlike anyone he'd ever known before. Not just because she hadn't gone to college or lived anywhere but Lone Star Canyon, but because she was smart and funny and incredibly compassionate. She was a woman who felt things deeply. Unfortunately, most of the men in her life had taught her to feel pain. Nora had just admitted that she knew the details of every failed marriage in the county. No wonder she preferred to be by herself.

Yet for one night she'd let him into her life and into her bed. She'd let him touch her and make her feel all of the possibilities. He knew that he wasn't supposed to fall in love again or care about a woman the way he'd cared about Courtney, but he couldn't help wishing that he and Nora could be more than friends. Of course if she was pregnant, they were going to be a whole lot more.

"I need to head over to the shop," she said, reaching in the back seat and grabbing her tote bag. "I have my first customer in less than a half hour."

He put his hand on her arm. "Not so fast, young lady. You and I have a date to take a pregnancy test."

Nora knew she was chattering like a magpie, but she couldn't seem to stop. Nerves, she thought as her mouth kept flapping away uncontrollably. She was terrified about the results of the test. Afraid she was pregnant and afraid that she wasn't.

"I can't believe you had me pee on a stick," she said, pacing in his office. "This is a medical center. Shouldn't things be more high tech?"

"I can draw blood if you'd like, but this test is accurate."

She glanced at the white plastic stick resting on a paper towel at the edge of the desk. Stephen sat in his big leather chair, apparently completely relaxed.

"I wouldn't let you near me with a needle," she told him. "And I don't want your nurse to know what's going on, so I guess the stick will have to do."

She crossed the beige carpet to stand by the window. "It's been pretty clear since the tornado, but I heard that there's a spring storm coming in tomorrow. I guess we need the rain. At least that's what they said on the radio this morning."

She folded her arms over her chest, trying not to think about what they were waiting for as she continued to babble about the weather. She felt so confused by everything about Stephen. She liked him. She liked him more than she'd liked any man in a long time. But he wasn't for her. She knew that. They didn't have very much in common. So it made sense to end the affair as quickly and quietly as possible. After all, the theory of a sex-based, no-strings affair had sounded really nice, but the reality was more than she could handle. So as soon as the pregnancy test came back negative, she would—

"It's done."

She turned on her heel and stared at him. He was looking at the white plastic stick, but she couldn't read the expression on his face.

"Stephen?"

He held out the stick to her. She crossed to his desk and stared at the pink plus sign. She was pregnant.

Baby? She was going to have a baby? She pressed a hand to her stomach, as if she could already feel the life growing inside of her. She waited for fear or regret or apprehension, but there was only bright, incredible joy. A child of her own. A wonderful, happy, healthy baby!

Stephen watched the dawning comprehension on Nora's face. He hadn't realized he was holding his breath until he allowed himself to exhale slowly. He'd half expected anger or resentment, but her expression held only a light of happiness he'd never seen before. It was as if she'd been granted her most secret wish.

"Aren't you thrilled?" she breathed, clasping her hands together and turning in a slow circle in the center of the room. "A baby!"

He felt himself smile, although his response was more contained than hers. While a part of him was pleased with the news, he was also concerned. With Courtney he'd had to temper his elation because she'd been so ambivalent. He'd anticipated the birth of a child before, only to have the tiny life lost almost before it had begun. Still, this was a second chance to be a father.

He dropped the stick onto the paper towel and thought how in less than nine months he would hold his child in his arms. Son or daughter, he didn't care.

"Isn't it amazing?" Nora practically danced over to the desk. Her entire face glowed. "I can't wait. I don't know the first thing about being pregnant. I guess I need to buy some of those books and I'll have to eat better, but, oh, isn't it wonderful?" She pressed her hands to his arm. "If you've changed your mind, I'm okay with that, too. I mean, I could be a great single mom. I have brothers and sisters to provide support, and my mom is going to be thrilled when I tell her."

He cupped her face in his hand. "Not in this lifetime, Nora. I meant what I said before. This child is as much mine as it is yours. We're getting married and we're going to be raising our baby together."

Even as he spoke the words, he couldn't believe he was saying them. But he knew he meant every syllable. He would marry her because it was the right thing to do. He wanted his child to have a stable home. He and Nora might not be wildly in love, but he figured they liked and respected each other. They could build a working relationship from that.

"But we don't have to get married," she told him. "If you want to be a part of things, we can co-parent or whatever. I'm not after your money. I don't need it or you. If you're doing this because you feel you have to—don't. Please. I'll be fine."

"But *I* won't be fine. I need my child and I won't let you deny me that." He wondered if it was possible for him to ever learn to need her as well. Courtney had taught him not to depend on a woman to make him happy—that she was more focused on her career than on their relationship. Would Nora be any different?

"You're being very backward," she protested, pulling away from his touch. "We don't have to decide anything right now."

"I'm not going to change my mind. If nothing else, you have to consider where we are. Lone Star Canyon is a small town. People will talk. I don't want that for you or for the baby.''

She opened her mouth, no doubt to argue, then closed it. Nora had had enough gossip to last her a lifetime. He doubted she would willingly sign up for more.

''As for time, we don't have as much as you think,'' he said. ''People can count backward and figure out about when all this started. So we need to get moving on getting married fairly quickly.''

Her gaze narrowed. ''You're trying to make this about me, but it isn't, is it? You're really concerned about your own reputation.''

''If you think so little of me, why did you make love with me?''

Their gazes locked in steady combat. She looked away first. ''I didn't think that…exactly.''

''Then what did you think?''

She sighed. ''Why are you being so difficult?''

''I could ask you the same question.'' He moved close and rested his hands on her shoulders. ''We have some time, but not as much as either of us would like. The bottom line is I'm going to be involved in my child's life and I want to be a real, full-time father, legally and otherwise. The only way I can do that is to live with my child. I doubt you're willing to give up custody to me, so the compromise is that we share the responsibility. Culturally that means getting married.''

''That's not my first choice,'' she said.

''Do you have a better suggestion?''

She was silent for a long time, which for Nora, was fairly rare. As she thought, he continued to rest his hands on her shoulders, enjoying the warmth of her so close to him. If nothing else they were going to have a great sex life, he thought, anticipating long nights of sharing a bed.

She stepped back. "I'm not saying yes."

"You don't have to...for now. But I'm not taking no for an answer."

She glanced at her watch. "I have to go. I have a customer due in any second."

"Promise me you'll think about my proposal."

Her mouth twisted in a wry smile. "It'll be hard to think about anything else." She headed for the door.

"Nora? I received an invitation to your brother's wedding. Would you go with me?"

She paused by the door, then nodded once before letting herself out. Stephen watched her go. She could fight him all she wanted, but the bottom line was they *would* be married long before the baby was born.

He told himself it was little more than a business transaction, to be completed for the sake of an unborn child. But a part of him was secretly pleased at the turn of events, and he had a sense of anticipation— as if he'd just been given an incredible and unexpected gift.

Chapter Twelve

Nora drove onto Darby land shortly after seven that night. She told herself that she was coming to see her mother because it had been more than a week since they'd had a chance to talk. But even as she pulled up in front of the familiar house, she found herself nearly bursting with the need to share what had happened in her life. Hattie was neither judgmental nor overbearing. She knew how to listen and advise with loving concern. Nora couldn't think of anything she needed more.

She turned off her engine and stepped out of the car. When she'd phoned earlier her mother had told her that Jack, Katie and Shane were spending the evening in town—having dinner, then going to a movie together. So she and her mother would have the house to themselves. Not that she was going to be able to keep her condition a secret from the rest of her family

for very long. Soon there would be the physical man-
ifestation of her pregnancy.

Nora jogged up the front steps and opened the door.
"It's me," she called as she walked inside.

Her mother appeared from the direction of the
kitchen and gave her a warm smile. "I'm so happy
to have you over tonight, Nora," she said, holding
open her arms to give her eldest daughter a hug. "I
always enjoy seeing you and spending time with
you."

Hattie, a vivacious brunette, with only a small
amount of gray in her long hair, had the energy and
figure of a much younger woman. She was shorter
than Nora, but they had similar dark eyes and easy
smiles. Tonight Hattie was dressed in jeans and a
long-sleeved shirt. The only evidence of her riding
accident a few months before was a slight limp.

Nora walked into her embrace and held her mother
close. The familiar strength and warmth made her feel
safe. "Hey, Mom," she said, closing her eyes and
wishing she were young again. Life had been so much
easier then. "What's for dinner?"

"Meat loaf and mashed potatoes. Your favorite.
When you called me earlier, you sounded as if you
needed a little pick-me-up."

Nora stepped back, intent on saying that she was
fine, but those words wouldn't come. Instead, she
found herself brushing tears from her cheeks and trying to hold in the sobs. "I really messed up, Mom."

Hattie didn't say anything. Instead she led her
daughter into the living room. When they were seated
next to each other on the sofa, Hattie took Nora's
hand in hers and squeezed gently. "Start at the beginning and tell me what's wrong."

Nora sniffed, then wiped her face with the fingers of her free hand. What was she supposed to say? But she desperately needed advice, so she was going to have to figure out something and fast.

"I've been seeing Stephen Remington," she said slowly, staring at her lap. She sniffed again. "Well, not exactly seeing. We're not a couple or anything. I mean, I guess we've dated a few times, but..." Her voice trailed off.

Hattie leaned toward her. "Honey, are you talking about sex? I have seven children of my own, so I'm familiar with the process."

Nora squeezed her eyes shut, then forced herself to look at her mother. Hattie's smile was supportive and understanding. "I hadn't thought about it that way. You would know a thing or two, wouldn't you?"

"I might." Her mother gazed at her. "So you and Stephen are lovers. As you're both single adults, I don't see the problem."

How to explain? "It's not that simple. You see, he said that he wasn't interested in getting involved. Romantically." She pulled her hand free of her mother's and leaned forward, resting her elbows on her knees. She had a bad feeling this was all going to sound really awful.

"You're saying he didn't want a commitment but he was interested in being intimate."

"Something like that. It wasn't supposed to be a one-night stand. We agreed to be monogamous. Sort of really, really close friends."

"All right. So where's the problem? Are you concerned that your feelings for him have changed? That you want to be more than friends and he doesn't?"

If only it were that simple, Nora thought. "Not exactly. The condom broke. I'm pregnant."

She risked glancing at her mother, half afraid of the censure she might see in Hattie's dark eyes. But when the older woman shrieked with pleasure and pulled her into a bear hug, Nora reminded herself that her mother had always been the kind of woman who gave with a full heart and rarely judged anyone.

"A baby!" Hattie crowed, holding Nora close. "I can't tell you how long I've been waiting for grandchildren. You'd think with seven kids of my own that one of you might have figured out how to procreate, but no. I had to raise an independent lot. At least with Jack marrying Katie I have Shane, but he's almost ten. I don't think he's going to let me hold him and rock him to sleep very much."

Nora straightened and looked at her mother. "You're sure you're not mad?"

"Oh, honey, I know this isn't what you wanted or expected, but I can't be sorry. Babies are miracles from God. You always said you wanted children. Have you changed your mind?"

"Not at all. I'm excited about the baby. The problem is Stephen."

Hattie lowered her arms to her side. "So he doesn't want the child. Is he pressuring you to terminate the pregnancy?"

Nora shook her head. "Just the opposite. He swears he wants to get involved from the beginning. He—" She cleared her throat because she barely believed what she was about to say. Actually speaking the words out loud might make them real enough to terrify her. "He says we should get married."

Her mother reacted calmly to the bombshell. Hattie

leaned back against the sofa and studied her oldest daughter. "I take it you're resisting his suggestion."

"Of course. It's crazy. Marriage? We barely know each other. This isn't the nineteenth century. We don't have to get married. I'm perfectly capable of supporting myself and my child. If he wants to be a part of the baby's life, then I guess we'll work something out. Couples do that all the time."

"I suspect he wants more than biweekly visits."

"Tell me about it. He's insisting that the only way he can truly share in the experience is for us to get married. Unless I'm willing to give him custody, which I'm not." She rested her elbows on her knees and her head in her hands. "It's just crazy. I want the child. What I don't want is a husband."

Her mother sighed softly. "Not every man is like your father or even David Fitzgerald. They don't all leave."

Nora winced. She hadn't meant to open old wounds. Not for herself and not for Hattie. "I know that. There are good men out there."

"I think you have intellectual knowledge, but I don't think you believe it in your heart. When your dad left, we all felt it, but as the oldest daughter, your perspective was different from everyone else's. I think Russell walking out on us taught you to be wary. If David had done what he'd promised, you would have realized that some relationships fail but others succeed. Unfortunately his leaving only reinforced what you'd already learned. From what I can tell, Stephen is one of the good guys. Maybe he deserves a chance."

Nora spun to face her. "You can't be serious. You're not telling me I should marry him."

"I'm saying you should think about it."

Nora didn't know how to respond. Marry Stephen? So she could spend the rest of her life being compared to his late wife and come up wanting? How was she supposed to compete with a perfect ghost? Courtney had been a doctor—a surgeon—who healed dying children. She, Nora, was a hairdresser. But she couldn't bring herself to tell her mother about Stephen's past. It was all too embarrassing.

"Next you'll be saying that the gossip will be a problem."

"It will," Hattie said evenly. "Lone Star Canyon is a small town. People talk. You've learned that lesson, too, Nora. You remember what happened when your father left. What about when a girl got pregnant in high school? Was society at large very forgiving?"

Nora slowly shook her head. She'd heard the whispers, sometimes the shouts. Her beauty shop was a microcosm for life in general, and she knew for a fact that gossip made the wheels of life turn.

"There's another reason you need to think about marrying Stephen," Hattie told her. "And this might be the most important reason of all."

Nora resisted the urge to roll her eyes. "I can't even guess what you're going to say now."

"Just that you're already in love with him, and if you don't take a chance on making this work, you're going to regret it for the rest of your life."

She hadn't thought anything could stun her more than finding out she was pregnant, but she'd been wrong. In love with Stephen? "That's not possible. In love with him? I don't even know if I like him."

Her mother didn't say anything, but she didn't have

to. Her wise brown eyes spoke volumes about one protesting too much.

In love? With him? It had been sex and nothing more. Just passion and the odd bit of conversation. All right, he was vaguely amusing from time to time and he didn't annoy her as much as other men did. She might have been oddly put out when she'd found out about Courtney, but that had been because she'd been concerned about being involved with someone who was in love with another woman. Her worries hadn't been about the state of her heart. Rather she'd been aware of potentially violating her moral code— she didn't have relationships with married men. That was all. She certainly hadn't been jealous.

"I don't love him," she said firmly. "I don't think I'm capable of loving a man. I gave that up a long time ago."

"You're speaking as if you think we get a choice in the matter. We don't. The heart has a mind of its own."

"Not my heart. It toes the party line."

But there was a sinking sensation in her stomach as she said the words and she had a horrified feeling that her mother might have gotten it right in one.

Wednesday evening Stephen sat on the steps of Nora's front porch. He hadn't seen her in four days. He'd left her phone messages, both at home and at work. He'd tried to corner her before she entered the shop and when she left. He'd even barged in this afternoon at two, expecting to find her working her magic on one of her clients. Instead her chair had been empty and he'd found himself backing out of the shop without bothering with an explanation.

The soon-to-be mother of his child was doing a damn fine job of avoiding him, but he wasn't going to let her continue any longer. He'd decided to park himself in front of her house for as long as it took. Eventually she would have to come home.

As he sat in the darkness of the spring evening, he wondered if she was nervous about being pregnant. The news had been unexpected for both of them, but while he would have nine months before his role became active, she was dealing with the reality of the baby every day. Even before the baby began to show, there would be physical manifestations only she could experience.

On his good days he allowed himself to be excited about the prospect of being a father. He'd dreamed the dreams before and had lost them all. For a while he'd lost himself as well. But he was working hard to convince himself that this pregnancy was different, so the outcome would be different. He already knew the mother was very different. Nora was many things, but she wasn't a replacement for Courtney.

They were both smart women, so the baby would probably be blessed with intelligence, but the likeness ended there. Courtney had been driven toward success to the exclusion of nearly everything else. Nora was more involved in her life. She had people around her whom she cared about. Despite the prickly exterior, she was soft and giving on the inside.

Physically the women were very different. He smiled at the thought of a little girl with Nora's flashing brown eyes and fearlessness. An image came to him—of Nora holding her baby tightly in her arms.

She would be a good mother. Practical, giving yet firm, teaching her child to believe that he or she could touch the stars. Hers would be a house of laughter and love. Then he wondered what role he would have in that house. Theirs would be a marriage based on practicalities.

Was that wrong? Stephen wasn't sure, but he knew he couldn't let her walk away. He had to be a father to the child—he had to be a part of the baby's life. There was an ache inside of him that wouldn't go away, nor would it let him abdicate his responsibilities. Which didn't answer the question of marriage. All he knew was that by being married to Nora, he could maintain the illusion of control.

He knew it was an illusion. He'd been married to Courtney and he hadn't been able to save her. He still remembered what it had been like when he'd arrived at the hospital where she'd been taken after she'd collapsed. He'd been too late to help, too late to be there as she breathed her last. Too late to tell her he was sorry. Instead he'd stood at her side and had taken her cool hand in his. He'd told her he loved her, even though she couldn't hear the words. He'd wanted to tell her that if only he'd known, he wouldn't have insisted.

But she was dead and there was to be no absolution for his sin. Instead he'd been led away to the room that held his tiny stillborn son. So perfect, so near to life, and yet gone. Stephen had touched the miniature fingers and toes, and he'd wept. Because he couldn't find it in his heart to be sorry that he'd wanted a child.

That was his greatest sin. That he might have insisted, anyway. So instead he'd promised her he would love her forever. That he would love only her, no matter what.

A sweep of headlights cut through his thoughts. He

glanced up and saw Nora pulling into her driveway. She turned off the engine and the lights, then stepped out into the night. He rose to his feet.

She didn't act surprised when she looked at him, so she must have seen him when she'd pulled in. She also didn't look especially happy.

"What do you want?" she demanded.

"We have to talk."

She headed toward him, then stepped past him to the front door. After opening it with her key, she turned back toward him. "I thought men were supposed to hate having conversations with women. I thought you all went out of your way to avoid anything remotely resembling an intimate discussion. But here you are, wanting to talk. Why is that?"

"You're just lucky."

Her eyebrows rose. "I can think of many ways to describe my condition, but that's not one of them." She jerked her head toward the interior. "You can come in if you'd like."

The invitation wasn't gracious, however Stephen figured it was the best he was going to get. He crossed the porch and stepped into the warm, welcoming house.

Nora had already tossed down her purse and stepped out of her shoes. She stood in the center of the living room, her hands on her hips. "Let me guess," she said, turning to face him. "You want to talk about getting married. Is the new plan to simply show up everywhere and wear me down?"

He couldn't help laughing. Trust Nora to cut to the heart of the situation. Whatever worries he might have about their life together, he didn't have to be concerned about being bored.

"I'll do what I have to," he told her. "Whatever it takes to get you to agree. We both know that getting married is the right thing to do."

He might know it, but she hadn't decided, Nora thought to herself as she glared at him. She hated how good he looked, just standing there. She'd decorated her house based on the assumption that she would spend her life alone. Feminine colors, ruffles, pillows and soft lines decorated nearly every room. Stephen should have looked out of place amid the English country floral print on her sofa and club chair, but he didn't. Instead he just looked tall, handsome and masculine.

She really hated that, although not as much as she hated how her heart had fluttered when she'd seen him waiting for her on her porch. She'd been avoiding him because she needed to figure out what she was feeling and what she was going to do. She didn't know either, yet, but she suspected he wasn't going to give her any more time.

Marriage. He wanted to marry her. Nora thought about all she and her mother had discussed a few days before. That it might be the best thing for the baby. That Nora might be falling in love with him. She could accept the former but she hated the latter. She didn't want to be in love with anyone. Not again. Love was a one-way ticket to the land of broken hearts and she didn't want to go there again.

There had to be a thousand other ways to make this situation work, she told herself as she met his hazel gaze. There had to be. Unfortunately, she had a bad feeling that her mother had been right. Which explained why her chest seemed to get tight every time she saw Stephen and how he made her crazy, but in a good way. But marriage. That was so extreme. And dangerous.

"I'll never be Courtney," she said, then pressed her lips together. She hadn't meant to say that, exactly.

Stephen took a step toward her. He'd obviously come straight from his office, because he was still dressed in a white shirt, dark slacks and a tie. She liked him in his business clothes. She also liked him in jeans, although her current preference was for him to wear nothing at all.

"I didn't expect you to be anyone but yourself," he said. "This isn't about anyone but us. You, me and the baby."

She wanted to believe him, but she had her doubts. She suspected one of the reasons he was insisting on being so closely connected with her and the child was that he'd already lost one family. He wanted to make sure that didn't happen again. She didn't blame him exactly, but she hated the comparison.

"Just because I'm not a doctor doesn't mean I'm any less a person," she told him.

He drew his eyebrows together. "What are you saying? This isn't about your intelligence, is it? You have to know you're one of the smartest people I've ever met. It has nothing to do with where you went to school—it's about who you are inside."

"I know that." She *did* know; she was just glad he'd figured it out, too.

She dropped her hands to her sides and walked over to the sofa. Once there, she perched on the edge of a cushion. "I have very definite ideas about marriage. Especially where men are concerned."

He joined her on the sofa, although he relaxed back

against the cushions as if this was an ordinary conversation. As if he didn't have a worry in the world.

"I'm aware that you have opinions about nearly everything," he said, his voice low and teasing. "I want to learn every one of them. So tell me about your thoughts on marriage."

"I only want to get married once. Having a child is a lifetime commitment. If your intent is to do this for a couple of years and then bail out—I'm not interested. To make this work, I expect you to stick around. The fact that you don't love me shouldn't have anything to do with it."

"Agreed," he said easily. "I had a long-term commitment in mind as well. I'm not looking to leave."

She swallowed. Thank goodness he hadn't caught her slip. Saying "you don't love me" was much more specific than saying "we don't love each other." But he hadn't noticed. She would have to be more careful. She didn't want him figuring out her secret.

He moved closer to her and cupped her face, gently forcing her to look at him. "I know you're scared, Nora. You have a history of men walking out on you. I want you to know I'm not like them. I don't know why your father ran off, but I'm certain it had nothing to do with you. As for David Fitzgerald—the man was an idiot. You're a prize and he should have seen that."

He rubbed his thumb over her mouth. "I didn't propose lightly, despite how it might have seemed. You're going to be a constant challenge. You're beautiful and sexy and funny and caring. I want to have a successful marriage based on affection and respect. I think we can manage that, don't you?"

She nodded because she couldn't speak. Not with

him touching her like that. Just the feel of his thumb on her mouth made her shiver all the way to her bones. His erotic stroking made it impossible to think. But she had to think. She had to be conscious of what he was saying and figure out how she was going to respond.

"You left one thing out," she told him, pulling away slightly so that he dropped his hand to his lap. "In addition to affection and respect, we'll also have sex."

He grinned. "I do expect that part of our marriage to be amazing."

His words should have pleased her but they didn't. She wanted more. She wanted it all.

Nora closed her eyes and tried to think. This was her reality. She was pregnant by this man and he was going to hound her until she gave in to him. Which meant they were probably going to get married. If she'd been able to walk away from her life and hide out somewhere for a couple of years she might have a chance at forgetting him. But that wasn't an option. So she would have to learn how to make peace with her decision and keep herself and her feelings safe.

"Say yes," he urged.

She looked at him. "If you leave me the way Russell left my mother, I'll hunt you down like the dog you are."

"I wouldn't expect any less. Say yes."

She hesitated. He was going to break her heart. He was going to shatter her and scatter the pieces to the winds. And there wasn't anything she could do about it.

"I don't want to say or do anything until after Jack

and Katie's wedding next week. I don't want to take away from their special day.''

"Is that a yes?"

She nodded slowly. "Yes, Stephen, I'll marry you."

He wrapped his arms around her and pulled her close. She found herself pressing against the familiar strength of his chest and reveling in the glory of being close to him. He felt wonderful and warm and everything she could have wanted.

His mouth came down on hers. The melting began instantly inside of her. Fire licked through her as she felt her resolve drain away. Gathering what little strength she had left, she pressed her hands against his shoulders and pushed.

"There will be none of that until after the wedding," she said firmly.

He looked as if he was going to protest, but instead he nodded. "If you insist."

"I think it's best." Mostly because she needed time to get herself together.

He took her hand in his and lightly stroked her fingers. "What do you want to do about a wedding? Something formal? We have a little time until people figure out the truth."

A wedding. She hadn't thought about the details of getting married. "Nothing big," she said. She couldn't face that. Not when they weren't marrying for the usual reasons. "Let's just fly to Las Vegas after Jack and Katie's wedding. That would be easiest. We'll tell everyone we eloped after we get back."

"Sounds like a plan."

He looked pleased—probably because he was getting everything he wanted. What about her? What did she want?

"Is this relationship going to be what you offered me before?" she asked. "Friendship and sex, only this time we'll be married and eventually parents. Is that what you expect?"

"What else would it be? Don't you think anything else would complicate the situation?"

"You're right, of course," she said, giving him her best smile.

But to her the future looked cold and empty. Living with and loving a man who would never love her back. Spending her life knowing she would always be his second-best wife.

Chapter Thirteen

The sound of soft music and laughter filled the Darby family room. Nora forced herself to keep smiling, reminding herself this event wasn't going to last forever...even if it felt like it.

At least the wedding had gone off perfectly. A spring storm had blown through in the night, making the eleven o'clock outdoor ceremony impossible. But Hattie had planned for that possibility. The furniture in the living room had been put out in the garage, leaving space for the ceremony. Garlands of fragrant flowers graced the tall windows and a long white cloth had defined the center aisle.

Nora smiled as she remembered the happiness in her brother's eyes as he'd taken Katie to be his wife. Shane, Katie's son, had beamed with pleasure at the thought of finally having a dad.

After congratulations and pictures, everyone had

moved into the family room where there were several round tables set for dinner and a buffet by the fireplace. A table in the corner held a beautiful four-tiered wedding cake, decorated with cascades of delicate violets.

"What are you thinking?" Stephen asked as he came up behind her and placed a hand on her waist.

"That my mother did a fabulous job pulling everything together in such a short period of time."

She allowed herself to lean against him, grateful for his physical and emotional support.

"I'm impressed," Stephen told her, speaking directly into her ear. "When I woke up and saw the rain I was concerned that everything might be ruined. Instead the arrangements are such that if I didn't know better I would assume this was the plan all along."

Nora nodded in agreement, then turned so she could watch her mother move through the room, speaking with her guests and making sure the event continued smoothly. Hattie paused by her new daughter-in-law and the two women laughed together.

They were a study in contrasts, Nora decided. Her mother with her thick, long dark hair and snapping brown eyes. Katie was petite, a blue-eyed, blond-haired china doll. As the bride she wore a fitted, cream-colored gown that fell to the floor. A scattering of seed pearls gave the silk texture and dimension. A beautiful diamond-and-pearl necklace rested on her collarbone, a gift from her new husband. From across the room Jack gazed at his bride, love shining from his eyes.

Nora tried to be pleased about all that had happened. But as much as she wanted her brother to be happy, she'd dreaded his wedding and the reception that followed. Darbys and Fitzgeralds occupying the same space was enough to make anyone nervous.

Aaron Fitzgerald had been true to his word—that he would never forgive his daughter for marrying a Darby. He hadn't bothered to respond to the invitation. But his wife, Suzanne, had arrived with their children Blair and Brent in tow. The teenagers looked anything but excited to be at their half sister's wedding, but they were polite to everyone.

Stephen tightened his hold on her waist. "I've met the enemy," he murmured.

She didn't know if she should cuff him or laugh. "You mean David?"

"Who else? There's nothing like meeting the 'other man' to make a fiancé feel protective."

He was teasing her to make her feel better and she appreciated that, but his words also made her heart ache just a little. Mostly because she wanted him to be speaking the truth. Stephen being jealous of David Fitzgerald would mean he cared about her as more than a bed partner and the mother of his child. An unlikely occurrence, she reminded herself.

"You don't have to worry," she told him. "David is a little too busy with his own life to even notice I'm here."

"Oh, I don't think that's true. I would say he's very aware of your presence, and my proximity. Good. Let him eat his heart out. He had his chance and he blew it."

She followed his gaze and saw the man in question talking to his wife. Fern was seven or eight months pregnant. David already had three girls. No doubt he was hoping for a boy this time.

As she studied David, she searched her feelings, wondering if any emotions lingered. She felt a small amount of regret that she'd been hurt by his marriage to another woman, but she didn't regret the loss of the man. With the hindsight of years, she wondered if they would have made each other happy. While she'd been raised on a ranch and was familiar with the requirements to keep it running, she found she preferred her life in town. Owning the beauty shop gave her a sense of pride. No matter what happened in her world, she would never need to depend on anyone to take care of her.

"Fern looks tired," Stephen said.

"You try having three small kids at home with a fourth on the way. We'll see how perky you feel."

He surprised her by grinning. "You never just have a conversation, do you? It's always a battle. You'll probably threaten my life on a regular basis, but I'll go laughing."

Before Nora could respond, Hattie clapped her hands to get everyone's attention.

"I have a special surprise," she said, moving to the television that stood against the far wall. "Someone very special wants to send the happy couple wedding wishes."

"Who is it?" Katie asked.

Jack only smiled at her. "You'll see."

They stood close together, their arms around each other. Nora glanced around the room. Monica, Tom and Wyatt had made it home from college for their big brother's wedding. Only Ivy and Keith hadn't been able to fly in for the ceremony. Ivy's son had an ear infection, which prevented them from flying in—and Florida was too far a drive for a weekend visit. Keith's work kept him out of the country.

Nora found herself wondering when was the last time the entire family had been together. Everything had changed so much from when they were kids. Keith was her twin, yet she rarely saw him anymore. He'd left for college nine years before and she doubted he'd been back even a half dozen times since. Ivy had been the same.

The television screen flickered as Hattie turned on the VCR. The camera wobbled a bit, then focused. Nora caught her breath as two familiar figures came into view. They were seated on a hospital bed, beside a bandaged figure.

"Hey, Katie and Jack, it's us, wishing you a happy wedding." Dallas Fitzgerald waved. She was a pretty young woman in her mid-twenties. A.J., Katie's younger brother, also raised his hand in greeting.

"Welcome to the 'better' family, Jack," he called out humorously. "So are you going to change your name to Fitzgerald?"

But Nora barely noticed them. Instead her attention focused on the bandaged figure in the middle. Dressings covered the woman's face and there was a cast on her left leg. Nora's chest tightened as she took in the equipment beeping in the background and the sterile hospital room.

"Hi, Katie and Jack," the woman said. "It's Josie. I know you can't tell because I'm currently pretending to be mummy-woman, but it's really me. I hope you will be very happy together. I love you both, and you, too, Shane. The doctor says you probably won't recognize me when I'm finished with my surgeries, but she's promised I'm going to be gorgeous, so that's something.''

On the video Dallas and A.J. both hugged their sister. They called out a few more greetings, but Nora was too shocked by her friend's appearance to listen.

As if he sensed her distress, Stephen put his hand on her shoulder. ''I know it looks bad, but she's getting better.''

''I hope so.''

Nora tried to reconcile the injured woman with the girl who had once been her best friend. She looked at the laughing Fitzgerald siblings on the video.

''Are we idiots to carry on the feud?'' she asked.

''Of course,'' Stephen told her. ''But you already knew that.''

She didn't respond to his statement. Instead she glanced toward David—the man who had broken her heart and humiliated her in front of the entire town. He was tall, blond and still very handsome. He was both strong and kind—characteristics she admired. As she watched him with his wife, she sensed a tension between them and knew they weren't happy together. At one time she might have been pleased to know his marriage wasn't working, but not anymore. They'd taken different paths. Eventually she might find out what had happened to make him marry someone else, but it no longer mattered the way it had. She was content to let him—and their past—go.

''I guess you're right,'' she said slowly. ''There's no reason for the families to keep fighting. Not after all this time. But try explaining that to Katie's father. Sometimes I think the feud is the most important part of his life.''

Stephen glanced at Shane, Katie's son and Aaron's

grandson. "Then he needs a different life. He's missing out on a lot by not being here. It's sad."

She agreed. But some things couldn't be changed and Aaron Fitzgerald was one of them.

"Time for lunch," Hattie said when the video had finished. "Everyone find your places, please."

She and Stephen made their way toward the round tables, reading place cards as they went. Nora noticed that David and his wife were at the other end of the room. Something else she had to thank her mother for. It was one thing to feel generous toward the man in her heart. It would be another to have to sit across from him and his wife at a meal.

As Stephen held out her chair, a ray of sunlight broke through the clouds and flooded the room. "An omen," he told her, taking the seat next to her. "But is it for them or for us?"

"Maybe both," she answered, trying not to notice the flutter of nerves in her stomach. After the wedding reception, she and Stephen were driving to Dallas, where they would fly to Las Vegas. Their own wedding was scheduled for later that evening. They would spend the night there and return late tomorrow.

"Are you sure you don't want to tell anyone what we're going to do?" he asked.

"I don't want to spoil Jack and Katie's day."

While she was a little concerned about her mother's reaction, she was more worried about what they were doing. Could she really marry this man, knowing that she was in love with him and that he didn't share her feelings?

"Are we doing the right thing?" she asked.

"Absolutely. Don't you dare back out on me now," he instructed.

"I won't." She knew she wouldn't, but she also hoped he was right. That getting married so suddenly wasn't going to be something they would both regret.

"Do you take this man to be your lawfully wedded husband?"

Nora swallowed against the lump in her throat. She stared deeply into Stephen's hazel eyes, searching for second thoughts or uncertainty, but there was only quiet contentment in his gaze. He seemed so sure. Was she really willing to be the only one to back out now?

"I do," she whispered.

"Are you exchanging rings?" the judge asked.

She was about to say they hadn't thought of that when Stephen nodded and pulled two ring boxes out of his suit jacket pocket. She blinked in surprise.

"When did you get those?" she asked, her voice low.

He grinned. "I made time."

He opened the first box and pulled out a plain gold wedding band. From the second he pulled a circle of fiery diamonds. Her breath caught in her throat as she stared at the stunning piece of jewelry, so elegant and unexpected.

"It's so beautiful. I don't know what to say," she breathed.

"Just keep saying 'I do.'"

The rest of the ceremony passed in a blur. Nora vaguely recalled reciting more words, then briefly kissing her new husband. Fifteen minutes later she was wearing her new ring, which felt awkward and unfamiliar. The paperwork was complete and they were on their way up to their suite.

"Did I mention how beautiful you are?" he asked when the elevator door closed behind him and the car started up.

She glanced down at her white wedding dress. She'd found the gown on sale at a shop in Dallas. It was sleeveless with a scoop neck. The satin basket weave bodice clung to her body from her breasts to her hips. From there, smooth satin fell to the floor in an elegant sweep. "I wasn't sure if you would be upset that I chose to wear something traditional, but I haven't been married before and I thought…" She cleared her throat. "I just didn't want to be married in a regular dress."

"I meant it, Nora. You're gorgeous."

She blushed, something that never happened. Rather than look at him, she studied her wedding ring. "I didn't expect anything like this. A plain gold band would have been fine."

"But you like this better."

She risked a quick glance at him. "Of course. Who wouldn't?"

"Good. That's what I wanted. To make you happy."

The elevator stopped on their floor. She wanted to ask if he really meant that, but couldn't think of a way without getting into territory that was dangerous. How could he want to make her happy without wanting to love her? But if she was going to go in that direction, he could have as easily asked her how she could have married him without loving *him.* Except she did love him, which made everything so complicated.

He placed his hand on the small of her back and

urged her toward the suite. Once there he used his card key to let them into the spacious lodgings.

The drapes had been pulled back from the floor-to-ceiling windows, offering a view of twinkling lights.

"How about something to drink?" Stephen asked.

He crossed to a bottle sitting in an ice bucket and pulled it free. She set her bouquet of white roses and stargazer lilies on the table by the sofa and nodded in agreement.

They were staying in a lovely suite at the Venetian Hotel. A sweeping foyer with a marble floor led to a bedroom with a canopied king-size bed. The bathroom—complete with double sinks, a huge glassed-in shower and a tub big enough for an armada—was slightly larger than her kitchen back home. Past the bedroom was a living room with a sofa and two club chairs. There was a round table with four chairs by the floor-to-ceiling windows.

"I would have offered you champagne, but under the circumstances..." Stephen smiled at her as he handed her a champagne flute filled with sparkling apple cider.

She took the glass from him and hoped he didn't notice that her fingers trembled. Married. They were really and truly married.

"To us," he said, raising his glass to hers. "Long life and much happiness."

"To us," she repeated, and took a sip.

The sweet apple taste fizzed on her tongue. She forced herself to swallow past the lump in her throat, then set her glass down on the coffee table.

From the moment they'd touched down in Las Vegas, everything about the evening had been magical and surreal. Stephen had arranged to have a limo waiting to take them the short distance to the hotel. Once she'd stepped into the multistory building, she'd had a real sense of being in Italy. Marble floors, gilded columns, incredible art reproductions on walls and ceilings all contributed to the ambience. The bellboy had told her there were gondola rides on the shopping level of the hotel.

Now they were alone in their luxury suite and she found herself terrified of her new husband. *Husband.* The word was strange and uncomfortable in her mind. She'd never thought that she would marry anyone, let alone marry under these kind of circumstances.

"What are you thinking?" he asked as he came up behind her and placed his hands on her bare shoulders.

His skin was warm, but his words made her shiver. She couldn't tell him what was on her mind. He would never understand and she wasn't about to explain.

"I'm nervous," she admitted, because that was probably enough of the truth to appease him.

Nervous and afraid she'd just made the biggest mistake of her life. Worse, she had told Stephen that they weren't going to be intimate until after the wedding, which was now, and she had a bad feeling he was about to take her up on her promise. She wasn't sure she could do that with him. Not without blurting out her feelings—something she'd sworn she would never do.

"I'm nervous, too," he whispered as he pressed several soft kisses along her neck.

"Liar."

"I'm not lying."

She'd pinned her hair up on her head in a cascade

of loose curls. He pushed aside the ones trailing against the nape of her neck and nibbled down her spine.

Despite her misgivings, anticipation began to fill her. Their lovemaking before had been amazing. There was no reason to think it wouldn't be again. As for confessing what was in her heart—she was going to have to learn to hide that part of her. He could never know the truth.

"You smell wonderful," he said as he turned her toward him. She allowed herself to move as he directed, then placed her hands on his strong shoulders. He still wore the navy suit he'd had on for Jack and Katie's wedding. Passion darkened his eyes and tightened his expression. She read his need and his desire. He might not love her but he wanted her. For now that would have to be enough.

She reached for his tie, but before she could begin unfastening the length of silk, he found the zipper in the center of her back and unfastened it. Nora hesitated before shrugging out of her gown. She'd gone all out on her wedding day lingerie. She wondered if her new husband would appreciate the effort.

With a graceful move, she let the dress fall to her feet, then she stepped out of the shimmering mound of satin. As Stephen stared, his mouth dropped open and his eyes glazed over. She raised her head slightly as she smiled. All right. So the obscenely expensive scraps of silk and lace had been worth it.

She wore a white lacy bra, cut low, with thin straps. A matching triangle scrap of silk served as panties. A slender garter belt hugged her hips and held up white stockings that had a seam down the back. White satin high-heeled pumps finished her ensemble.

Stephen gathered his composure enough to close his mouth and swear. "Where do you buy something like that?"

"You like it?"

"Oh, yeah."

She turned to show him that the back of the panties was little more than a skinny elastic strap. "The set comes in other colors."

He swallowed visibly. "Great."

He reached up and fumbled with his tie. As she sauntered over to the bed, he trailed after her, dropping items of clothing like so many breadcrumbs. Some of her confidence returned. At least she knew she had his attention.

At the edge of the bed she paused, waiting for him to catch up. He'd removed his jacket, shirt and tie and was tugging off his shoes and socks. His arousal was clearly visible under the lightweight wool of his slacks. But instead of finishing his undressing, he straightened and looked at her.

"You're beautiful," he said simply.

"Thank you."

"I want you."

She gave him a slight smile. "I guessed that part."

"Tell me you want me, too."

For a second there was a flash of vulnerability in his eyes. Whatever lingering reservations she might have had faded at that moment. She moved close to him and wrapped her arms around him.

"More than I should," she breathed, and raised her mouth to his.

Their first kiss was hot and passionate. There was no time for gentle exploration—not with the fire flaring so brightly it threatened to blind them. She parted her lips as soon as their mouths touched and he immediately plunged his tongue inside her. He tasted sweet—like the apple cider, and yet like himself. She remembered his flavor, how she had savored his taste, his scent, even the way he moved against her.

His hands slid up her arms, then down her chest to cup her breasts. Instinctively she surged against him, desperate for more contact between them. His thumbs found her already tight nipples. He teased the sensitive tips, brushing against them over and over until she couldn't breathe.

"Don't..." she insisted.

"Don't what?"

"Don't stop."

The last word ended on a gasp as he bent low and nipped her breast through the lace of her bra. A shudder raced through her as her heart rate increased. Her body felt hot all over. Every inch of her skin had been sensitized to his touch. Magic. He was magic and she didn't want this ever to end.

He slowly lowered himself to his knees, all the while trailing kisses down her belly. When he reached the triangle of silk covering her feminine place, he tugged it along the length of her legs, then supported her while she stepped out of it.

"Sit down," he urged, and she did as he requested.

She knew what would happen next. She caught her breath in anticipation even as she stretched out on the bed with her legs still hanging off the side.

He stroked her legs from ankle to thigh. The layer of sheer silk added an erotic element to his touch. Up and down, up and down, never getting very close to the apex, leaving her hungry and restless.

"Touch me," she breathed. "Touch me like you did before."

He did as she requested. As his hands continued to slid up and down her legs, his mouth covered her most private place. His tongue sought and found that tiny point of pleasure and he traced it, circling slowly, deliberately. He gave her long, slow licks and short, fast, teasing flicks. Touching, not touching, kissing, nibbling, blowing lightly, then sliding two fingers into her.

He kissed her from above and stroked her from below, focusing all of his attention on her pleasure. Slowly at first, then moving faster and faster until she was out of control and gasping for breath.

Her release was unexpected. One second she'd been reaching, straining, muscles tense and shaking. The next she was falling, every cell in her body giving itself up to the moment of sheer perfection. Emotions worked to the surface, but she held them in by a supreme force of will. Words hovered on the tip of her tongue, but when she would have spoken them, she reached for him and drew him up, kissing him instead.

And then they were on the mattress, touching each other. Her hands were everywhere. She needed to be close to him, to pleasure him as he'd pleasured her. He pulled off his slacks and briefs, exposing his heavy arousal. She couldn't help rubbing him lightly.

He groaned as she stroked up and down along his length.

"You're going to kill me," he muttered, shifting onto his back and urging her to straddle him.

She still wore the garter belt and stockings. As she slowly lowered herself onto him, he found the hook holding her bra in place and unfastened it. His hands cupped her curves just as she took all of him inside of her.

He was large and thick, filling her completely. Her first instinct was to move, but she also wanted to enjoy the sensation of being so connected with him. They stared into each other's eyes, then she bent down and he stretched up as they kissed.

His hands slipped to her hips, urging her to move. She did as he silently requested, sliding up and down, making them both groan. She was still swollen and sensitive from her recent release. The feel of him inside of her was too intense and she felt herself collecting for another climax.

As if reading her mind…or perhaps her body…he deepened the kiss at the same time he cupped her breasts. Long fingers held her curves and stroked her nipples. It was more than she could stand. She tightened around him and cried out as pleasure filled her.

Involuntarily she quickened the pace. They continued to kiss, his hands moved on her breasts. Between her thighs, the magic occurred again. With each deep thrust she found herself falling into pleasure, over and over until she felt as if she'd lost control of her body. He was making this happen and she never wanted him to stop.

Finally he gave one last deep surge and was still. She shuddered around him, drawing his release from him, making them both gasp and cry out in a moment of perfect connection.

Later, when they'd both caught their breath and he'd finished undressing her, Stephen drew Nora under the covers and settled next to her. He held her cradled in his arms, enjoying the feel of her body next to his. Their lovemaking had been extraordinary—just as it had been the first couple of times. But there had been a different element. Was it because they were married?

He told himself that didn't matter. He hadn't married Nora because he loved her but because it was the right thing to do for their child. He hadn't really broken his promise to Courtney—the one he made on her deathbed when he'd sworn to never love anyone else.

The familiar guilt filled him, reminding him that all the promises in the world wouldn't bring Courtney back to him. She had died because he'd insisted she have the baby. As always, the reality of the situation confused him. If he hadn't insisted, she would have gotten rid of the baby—so he still would have had that death on his hands. He couldn't find his way out of the circumstances in such a way that everything worked out right.

He told himself he had to find a way to let the past go. He had a new life now. A part of his heart would always be devoted to Courtney and his son, but there were other souls to consider.

Nora lay curled up next to him, her head resting on his shoulder, her knee on his thigh. He stroked the arm resting on his chest.

"Have you thought about where we're going to live?" he asked.

She raised her head and looked at him. Confusion darkened her eyes. "No. But it's something we have to discuss. I hadn't realized there would be changes, but I guess that happens when one gets married."

"Usually." He dropped a kiss on the top of her

head. "My place is too small, especially with a baby on the way. Yours would be all right until the birth. I was thinking that we should buy a house together."

A smile tugged at her mouth. "I guess separate residences are out of the question."

"Absolutely. You're my wife and I intend to keep you firmly under my control."

Well-shaped eyebrows rose toward her hairline. "You can't be serious."

"Not for a second. But I do want us to live together."

She settled back on his shoulder and sighed. "All right. If you can stand a few weeks of lace and frills, why don't you move into my place while we start house-hunting for something we both like."

She said all the right things, but he felt her tense as she spoke.

He turned, rolling her onto her back. He pressed one hand against her still-flat belly, as if he could feel the tiny life growing inside.

"I know this isn't how you planned things," he said. "But if we have the same goals and expectations, we can make our marriage successful."

"You want to draw up a five-year plan?"

"Maybe. In the meantime I want to do whatever it takes to make you happy."

She looked away. "Be careful with words like that. They might go to my head."

Her voice sounded strange as she spoke, but he couldn't figure out what was wrong. "Nora, I hope you know that I care about you very much. You're a special woman and I'm happy to have you in my life. I think we're going to enjoy many good years together."

She swallowed, then gave him a teasing smile. "You sure know how to sweep a girl off her feet."

Something was bothering her, but he didn't know what. Had he said something he shouldn't? Did she want—

But before he could figure out what she might or might not want from him, she drew his hand from her belly to her breast. "Kiss me," she whispered.

The feel of her soft skin and the temptation of her mouth was too much. He bent toward her, all thoughts of conversation forgotten.

Chapter Fourteen

"Are you mad?" Nora asked her mother the following Monday morning.

She'd called Hattie when they'd arrived back from Las Vegas the previous night and her mother had met her at the shop first thing that morning.

Hattie sat in one of the straight-backed chairs in the waiting area. As usual she was dressed in jeans and a shirt, looking far younger than her fifty-plus years. She gazed at her daughter. "I'm not angry at all."

Nora believed her, but she still felt compelled to explain her reasons for eloping. "We knew we had to move quickly, because of the baby and all and I didn't want to take away from Jack and Katie's day."

"Of course you didn't." Her mother gave her a warm look. "Despite your reputation for being prickly, you're actually a very softhearted woman.

I'm pleased you and Stephen decided to get married. I think it's the right thing to do. However, I want you to be sure this is what *you* want.''

Nora twisted the diamond band on her left hand. The ring was still unfamiliar, but then so was being married. She thought of fifteen different ways to hedge the truth, then figured there wasn't much point.

''I'm not sure,'' she admitted. ''About anything. The only thing I absolutely know is that I want to have this baby.''

''You're doing that, so you should be happy.''

Nora smiled at her mother. ''Yes, but there's a six-foot man who wants to tag along. He's the something I don't know what to do about. I haven't told him how I feel because he doesn't want to hear it.''

Hattie picked up her daughter's left hand and studied the diamond ring. Nora knew that her father had given Hattie a simple gold band on their wedding day and that she'd worn it until just a few years ago.

Nora remembered being a little girl and finding out that her father had walked out on his family. Everyone had been devastated, but her mother had kept them all together, focusing on the future and their feelings for one another. She hadn't let the family fall apart. Not even when money was tight and cattle prices falling.

''Love is a tricky thing,'' Hattie told her, squeezing her fingers then releasing them. ''Our hearts don't always listen to reason, but our heads have to. Sometimes there's a battle. Do what's best for the baby, but also what's best for you, Nora. You have a responsibility to look out for yourself.''

''I know.'' She turned her mother's words over in

her mind. "For now I guess the best path is to try being married to Stephen."

"I agree. So give him a chance to be a good husband. I know a little about his past—that he was married before."

Nora was surprised. "He told you that?"

"Yes. When he was first treating me." Her mother shrugged. "I was feeling sorry for myself after my riding accident. I think he shared his past to snap me out of my self-pity. Hey, it worked." She touched her daughter's arm. "The point is he's done the husband thing before. I suspect he's going to feel some guilt and confusion about what is and isn't allowed in your relationship. It will take him a while to get used to being part of a couple again. Give him that time. He has a lot to offer both you and the baby. If you give up on him too soon, I suspect you'll regret it for the rest of your life."

Nora knew that her mother's advice was sound, but she didn't know how long she could live with being second best. Worse, in a battle between herself and Courtney, she was never going to win. How could she compete with a brilliant surgeon who was also petite and pretty and dozens of other wonderful things? If Courtney hadn't died, Stephen would still be happily married to her.

"He'll be a good father to your child," Hattie said.

"I know. That's one of the reasons I married him. I know he's a good man. I just don't know if he's willing to be the right one for me."

Her mother opened her mouth to say something else, but before she could speak, the front door of the shop flew open and a half dozen women charged into the reception area. Jill and Kathy led the way, followed by several clients. Mrs. Arnold, Mrs. Gelson and even Myrna Nelson stood beaming at her.

"We all heard," Jill said, stepping forward and giving her a hug. "Congratulations."

Nora wondered who had started the rumor. "News travels fast around here."

"Especially good news," Myrna said, moving past Jill to offer her own hug. "I knew something was up when the two of you came to visit me. Sparks were flying all around my kitchen." She arched her penciled brows. "I'm happy for you, my dear. You're a sweet girl and you deserve some happiness."

The sincere words brought tears to Nora's eyes, but she blinked them back. She accepted the good wishes from all the women, then urged Jill and Kathy to move to their stations and start the day. Hattie rose to leave.

"Good luck with all the talk," her mother said. "I'll forgive you for eloping as long as you promise to bring your new husband to dinner tomorrow night."

"We'll be there."

She waved and watched her mother leave. Then she turned to find several pairs of eyes focused on her. The salon went silent. Nora raised her hands in a gesture of surrender. "Go ahead. Start with the questions. The sooner we begin, the sooner they'll be done."

But they weren't going to be done anytime that day, she realized by midafternoon. It felt as if everyone she knew in town stopped by to offer congratulations and find out a few more details. She'd explained about her dress, the wedding ceremony itself, the beautiful hotel and her flowers. She'd had women coo over her impressive ring and ask when they were going to start a family.

"I think I should learn to be a wife before I worry about being a mom," she said as she applied a final coat of hair spray to Mrs. McDirmity's blue-white hair.

"It's so romantic," the elderly woman said as she leaned against the arms of her wheelchair. "I remember the day of the tornado. I thought even then there was something between the two of you."

Nora wasn't sure what that something could be. She was just grateful that they'd stopped talking about them having children. She knew it was only a matter of time until her condition showed, but with a little careful planning, that day was several months away.

"You've found a winner," Mrs. McDirmity insisted. "Stephen is very much in love with you. Everyone can see it."

Nora smiled but didn't say anything. After all, she knew the truth.

Stephen carried his coffee into the living room and selected the least pillow-filled chair. He'd been living in Nora's house for nearly two weeks and he still wasn't used to the lace, frills or scent of candles that filled the small rooms. Her house was an ode to the feminine. He should have felt awkward and out of place. Instead he found himself enjoying the contrast between this and his stark bachelor apartment. Even his house with Courtney hadn't been decorated with more than furniture and lamps. They'd never had time to make it a real home.

He set his coffee on an end table, then opened the

folder he'd brought in with him. "We need to talk about houses," he said.

Nora barely glanced up from the large baby paraphernalia catalog she was flipping through. He'd studied it himself over breakfast and it covered everything from cribs to pacifiers. "We haven't settled on baby names."

"I think a house is a more pressing issue," he told her. "The baby isn't going to be here for seven plus months. But if we're going to have a house built, we should get started right away."

She looked at him and smiled. "What? You want to leave my place? I thought you said you adored my frills."

What he adored was her, he thought as he shook his head. She was the most amazing woman he'd ever known. Smart and sexy as hell. Even when she wasn't trying.

Nora could get his blood boiling with the scraps of silk and lace she liked to tempt him with, but just being around her turned him on more than she would ever know. Tonight she wore jeans and a cropped T-shirt. The wide neck kept sliding down one shoulder, exposing her bra strap. When she stretched, he caught a glimpse of bare belly. It was all he could do to stay in his seat when what he wanted was to slide his arms around her and pull her close.

He knew that they were in the throes of sexual chemistry. In time the urge to make love would settle down into something more manageable. But he also sensed the need to be with her would never go away. There was a connection between them that he'd never experienced before—not with anyone else.

He shook off the heat in his blood and ignored the

heaviness in his groin. "We have to get serious about
the house. While I do like the frills and lace around
here, the place is too small." He held up two flyers,
each featuring a house they'd liked. "Pick one."

She returned her attention to the catalog. "They're
both fine." She turned a page and her breath caught.

"I don't want you to live in a house that's just fine.
I want you to love it. Is there one you liked better
or—"

He froze, then let the papers fall to the floor. Nora
sniffed as a single tear rolled down her cheek.

"Honey, what's wrong?" he asked as he moved
toward her and gathered her in his arms.

"N-nothing. Just this."

She held out the catalog to him. The open pages
showed a pink-and-white nursery with a fuzzy teddy
bear mobile over the crib.

He didn't understand. "Why would that make you
cry?"

"It's so c-cute."

More tears fell, faster now. He hugged her close as
he realized as a result of her pregnancy, she was being
flooded with hormones.

"It's all right," he murmured. "You'll feel better
soon. The chemicals in your body are making you
emotionally unstable. But it will pass."

She jerked away and glared at him. "Emotionally
unstable?"

He recognized the deep, dark pit, but it was too
late to avoid falling to the bottom. "That was a little
harsh," he said, backpedaling as fast as he could.
"The first trimester is a time of great change in your
body. This is manifested in many different ways."

Her gaze narrowed. "Don't think your doctor double-speak is going to save you. You said emotionally unstable and now you have to be punished.''

Not knowing how else to save the situation, he murmured, ''Yes, dear'' as meekly as he could, then pulled her close to him again.

She went grudgingly, but gradually she relaxed.

''Don't think I'm fooled by your attitude,'' she said, leaning her head against his shoulder. ''You are trying to be accommodating, but that's not your nature.''

''I can't fool you by tiptoeing around you?''

''Not for one second.''

He stroked her long hair. ''So why are you resisting putting an offer on a house? Is it because moving out of this place signals starting a new life and you're not comfortable with that?''

She sighed. ''I'm not really thrilled about you being insightful, either.''

He chuckled. ''Okay. I'll try to avoid that in the future.'' He kissed her temple. ''We can wait on the house until you're comfortable with the idea.''

He inhaled the sweet scent of her body and knew that he wanted her again. However, with her emotions so close to the surface, he wasn't sure how she would respond to his suggestion that they make love.

She sniffed and he realized she was crying again. ''What's wrong?'' he asked.

''Nothing.'' She raised her head and looked at him. Tears glistened in her eyes. ''You're just being really nice. I hate that. I like the house with the master suite downstairs. But I'll want the baby to be in the sitting area for the first few weeks.''

''That's fine.''

''No, it's not. I hate crying. I hate getting weepy

looking at a catalog. I hate that you've figured out that leaving here is going to be hard for me.''

"At least you don't hate me.''

She glared again. "Don't push me on that.''

He couldn't help laughing. "Like I said, Nora. You'll never be boring. The hormones will settle down and you'll be less emotional. Don't sweat it.''

She pushed away from him. "Easy for you to say and sit in judgment. It's not your body, is it? And aren't the rules interesting. Emotions are allowed as long as they're the result of the baby.''

He sensed more danger and told himself to step very carefully. The problem was he couldn't see the pit and might not until he was already falling into it.

"What are you talking about?'' he asked, keeping his voice as calm and reasonable as possible.

She sprang to her feet and planted her hands on her hips. "Don't worry. I'm not about to fall in love with you. I may not be a doctor like Courtney, but I'm not stupid.''

He felt as if she'd slapped him. Until that moment he hadn't thought about either of them being in love with the other. But as soon as Nora said the words, he knew that was what he wanted. He desperately needed her to love him. Nora would give her heart the way she lived—unselfishly and with her whole being. She would be sweet and tender and as protective as a mother tiger.

"Is that what you think I want?'' he said, standing. "A marriage without love?''

"You've made your opinion very clear from the beginning.''

She crossed to the far side of the room, stood behind a chair and faced him. The physical barrier in front of her told him of her need to feel safe and protected. He ached to go to her.

"Love is complicated," he admitted.

"Because of your late wife."

He nodded. "I have some unresolved issues about Courtney. I loved her and she died."

Her gaze focused on his face. "So what does that mean? You're not allowed to love anyone else?"

"Something like that." He thought about telling her about what had happened when Courtney died, but he suspected she wouldn't understand. "But that doesn't mean we can't care about each other."

"Oh, caring. Wow. I feel very special."

He was making matters worse but didn't know how to fix things. "What do you want me to say?"

"You don't have to say anything. Just tell me the truth. Which is what you're doing. I really appreciate that. I'm so excited to be married to a man who doesn't expect me to love him."

"You can if you want to," he told her, then felt awkward. "You don't have the same restrictions."

Her eyes widened. She slapped her hands on the back of the chair and glared at him. "Let me see if I get this straight. You're not going to love me because of your late wife, but golly, wouldn't it be grand if I fell in love with you? Of course. How incredibly perfect and just like a slimy, toad-sucking excuse for a man. How dare you?"

He took a step toward her. "Nora, that isn't what I meant."

"Yes, it is. And I can't really blame you. After all, who doesn't want to be loved by the multitudes. It's not enough that your patients adore you. No, now you want me to hand over my heart. Not that you're going to give me a piece of yourself in return. After all, you have to save yourself for the ever-wonderful Courtney. I'm just some woman you married who is having your baby. Not anyone special at all.''

He'd hurt her. He saw the pain in her eyes and heard it behind the anger in her voice. ''I'm sorry,'' he said, not sure exactly what had caused the pain. He didn't have a choice in loving Courtney. Couldn't Nora see that?

''Sorry? That hardly helps. You expect me to spend the rest of my life being second best. Well, you can forget that. I'm not interested in never measuring up. I'm not going to sit around here and wait for you to realize that I'm a hell of a woman and you're damn lucky to have me in your life.''

''You're not second best. Why would you think that?''

She stared at him. ''Because you've said it every time you've explained that you're not interested in loving me back.''

She turned and headed for the bedroom, then paused at the entrance to the hallway. ''Don't follow me, don't try to talk to me. My emotionally unstable hormones and I don't want to have anything to do with you right now.''

''But we have to talk.''

''Actually, we don't.''

And then she slammed the bedroom door shut, leaving him standing in the living room, confused and alone.

Chapter Fifteen

If there had been a way for Nora to turn back time the next morning, she would have sold her soul to do it. She still wasn't sure what had happened the previous night. One minute she'd been a normal, articulate person, the next she'd been fighting irrational tears and confronting Stephen about his relationship with his late wife.

She hated what she'd said to him because of what it revealed about herself. She'd never meant to tell him that she didn't want to be second best to Courtney and she certainly hadn't planned to share that she wanted him to love her.

If only the catalog hadn't made her cry. Or if only he hadn't figured out that she was ambivalent about leaving her small house and getting a larger one with him. Or if only he hadn't been so nice about that—

getting angry instead of saying she should take as much time as she needed.

She walked into the kitchen and turned on the light. It was early, barely past six, and Stephen was still asleep in their bed. She'd escaped to the bedroom after their argument. He hadn't joined her until well after midnight. She'd pretended to be asleep and he'd let her. They'd turned away from each other, trying to ignore the fact that there was little more than a foot or two of mattress between them.

Now she flipped on the coffeemaker for him and started water for her herbal tea. Her life had gotten very confusing. She wanted to blame everything on her wayward hormones, but she knew it was more than that. She had married a man she loved, knowing that he didn't love her back. She'd even told herself she understood that he might *never* love her back. She'd thought she was okay with that fact. But now she wasn't so sure. The thought of spending the rest of her life loving him while he loved Courtney made her sad. It also made her think the marriage had been a mistake.

This was her first marriage—the culmination of her girlhood dreams. But it wasn't like that for him. His reality was Courtney. What did that leave her?

"Good morning."

She turned and saw Stephen standing in the doorway to the kitchen. He'd just woken up and his hair was still mussed. He'd pulled on a navy terry-cloth robe, but his feet were bare.

"Hi," she said quietly, then nodded to the coffeemaker. "That should be ready in about two minutes."

"Good. I didn't get a lot of sleep last night and

I'm going to need the caffeine to get my brain work-ing.''

He walked over to lean against the counter. She told herself that she had to learn to harden her heart against this man, but she couldn't summon the strength. He looked sexy first thing in the morning. The stubble on his jaw seemed to blur his features a little and his gaze wasn't quite so sharp.

She'd already showered and dressed. She shoved her hands into her jeans pockets and wished her water would boil so that she would have something to do. Unfortunately the kettle remained silent.

She glanced at the tie on his robe, then at the floor, which could use a good scrubbing.

"Nora, I'm sorry about last night."

So he was going to talk about it. She'd wondered if he would. Some men didn't like to talk about prob-lems, instead ignoring them in the hopes that they went away. Just her luck that Stephen was one of the other kind.

"You have nothing to apologize for," she said, meeting his gaze. "You told me what you thought. That's not a punishable offense."

"But I hurt you and I was an insensitive jerk."

"You clarified the rules. I wouldn't want any less."

The fact that she hated those rules was her problem, not his. If only she didn't love him, things would be easier. They could have the relationship he'd sug-gested—warm, caring friends who were parents and lovers. But having fallen in love with him, she didn't think there was a way to un-love him.

He took a step toward her. "What aren't you telling me? I keep getting this sense of having a different script than you. As if we're not talking about the same thing.''

''I have no idea what you mean.''

It was a flat-out lie, which made her uncomfortable, but she wasn't ready to push back on the issue, nor was she going to confess her feelings. Stephen already had too much power in their relationship.

The kettle began to whistle, giving her a good excuse to turn away. While she busied herself with pouring water and dunking the tea bag, he grabbed a mug and served himself a cup of coffee. When they were both finished, she reluctantly returned her attention to him.

''If we don't talk, we're doomed,'' he said. ''I learned that from my first marriage.''

His reference to Courtney made her skin crawl. ''Because Miss Perfect did everything right?''

The comment was bitchy and made her feel small. She pressed her lips together. ''Sorry, Stephen. That just slipped out. I'm not trying to be rude.''

He shrugged off her apology. ''I know this is complicated for both of us. We're fighting with my past. But to address your comment, neither Courtney nor I was very good at communicating when there was a problem. Our work schedules allowed us to hide behind long hours. I don't want you and me to do the same. If we don't talk, our marriage isn't going to work.''

Nora had her doubts about it working, regardless, but she didn't say that.

He crossed the kitchen and put his hands on her shoulders. ''I care about you, Nora. Is that going to be enough?''

She looked into his hazel eyes. Before meeting Stephen she'd always thought that David Fitzgerald marrying someone else had been the low point of her life. Now she wasn't so sure.

"I don't know," she said honestly. "I'll have to get back to you on that one."

Stephen glanced at his schedule for the day and saw that he was finished with appointments until after lunch. He sorted through the pile of mail on his desk, then glanced toward the window. Although he didn't look out over the street, he always thought he might catch a glimpse of Nora as she left her shop to run an errand. He never did.

Tossing the unopened envelopes onto the desk, he sank back into his leather chair and closed his eyes. What was he going to do with his wife? It had been a week since they'd had the huge fight about his statement that it was okay for her to love him, without him feeling that he had to love her back. On the stupid scale of one to ten, that was a definite eleven. Maybe even a twelve. He'd sounded pompous, stuck-up and incredibly insensitive. He hadn't meant to be any of those, but his intentions wouldn't necessarily matter to Nora. She was more concerned with actions.

She confused the hell out of him. He liked her. Hell, at times he adored her. She was everything he could want in a wife. Except she needed things from him he couldn't provide.

The logical side of his brain told him that her wanting him to do more than care made perfect sense. Most marriages were based on mutual love. It was an expectation of the institution. But he couldn't do that. Love was not allowed. Maybe if Courtney hadn't died, if their marriage had continued on its course, it would have eventually ended on its own and things could be different. Maybe if he'd been able to—

His brain slammed to a halt as he replayed his last thought. The one that admitted that things hadn't been perfect between him and Courtney. He opened his eyes and stared unseeingly around the room. If Courtney hadn't died, would the two of them have divorced? Did he really think that?

Images from the past flashed through his brain. He and Courtney had rarely fought because they didn't spend very much time together. How could they when he was working impossible hours at the ER while she was focused on completing her residency and trying to land her fellowship? He remembered their celebration when she'd finally received notification that she'd been chosen. They'd had a wonderful dinner out, complete with champagne and toasts to the future. Three days later she'd learned that she was pregnant.

Stephen didn't want to remember that day, but he couldn't push away the memories of her angry statements that she didn't want to have the child. It wasn't a good time—she wasn't ready. He'd been horrified that she'd wanted to terminate her pregnancy because it wasn't convenient. He hadn't understood how she could walk away from a life they'd made together.

He remembered looking at her and wondering if he'd ever known her. He'd told her that if she didn't have the baby, he was leaving her.

Stephen gripped the arms of his chair. It had taken a threat of divorce to force Courtney to agree to carry the baby to term. Looking back with the wisdom of hindsight, he wondered what would have happened if he hadn't insisted. She would have gotten rid of the baby and he would have...

He would have left her. He knew that he couldn't have stayed with her under those circumstances. If she'd been young and unable to support herself or a child, if she'd been victimized or there had been a life-threatening condition, he would have understood her desires. But inconvenience was not an excuse. Not when they were both healthy, well-employed and more than capable of providing for an infant.

All of which had nothing to do with Nora, he reminded himself. So why was he wasting time thinking about this?

He shook off the memories and reached for his mail. As he flipped through the envelopes, he frowned when he saw one from his former boss back in Boston.

He pulled out the two-page letter and scanned the contents. Neil Edwards had been made chief of staff and wanted to offer Stephen a job as head of his emergency room. The job came with a great salary, bonus plan and plenty of perks.

You've got to be tired of living in the sticks, his friend wrote. *Come back to the real world, where you belong.*

Move back to Boston? Neil had never understood his desire to be a small-town physician. Not many people had, including Courtney. She considered his brief attempt to specialize in family practice as his rebellious streak. Something he'd outgrown.

Now, as he read the letter again, he knew he didn't want to go back to Boston. Not now, not ever. His life was here, in Lone Star Canyon. He knew most of his patients by name. He had a practice that was eclectic and varied. There was a sense of community and he wanted to be a part of that. Plus, he had a wife who lived here and he figured it was unlikely she would be willing to relocate to the East Coast.

He smiled as he imagined her reaction to the offer. She would be unamused, to say the least, but she wouldn't be quiet about it. She would probably tell him that she didn't intend to have her child grow up in a place where people were packed together like sardines, and that if she'd wanted to waste her life in a big city, that's what she would be doing. She didn't need him or any man rearranging her world, thank you very much.

He folded the letter and dropped it into his open briefcase. She was quite a woman. He hadn't known her very long, but he couldn't imagine living without her. He knew that he'd been an idiot to tell her that he wouldn't mind if she fell in love with him. Talk about self-absorbed.

Yet even as he knew it was wrong, a part of him wished that she would care about him that much. Nora in love would be irresistible. He was selfish enough to want to have some of her considerable attention focused on him. But that wasn't likely to happen. Although they'd made peace in the past couple of days, they were living under truce conditions. The easy laughter and passion of the first few days of their marriage had yet to be restored.

A knock on his office door caught his attention. He looked up and saw Myrna Nelson standing in the doorway. She wore a pink-and-white floral print dress and had on makeup and earrings. Her hair was freshly set. She patted her white curls and gave him a saucy smile.

"I just wanted to let you know that I might be a little late for our appointment later this afternoon. I'm having lunch with a friend."

"I'm glad you're getting out, Myrna. I like a woman who keeps her promises. But I thought you'd already had lunch with your lady friends."

Her expression turned coy. "I have. That was last week. Today I'm having lunch with a gentleman friend." Her eyebrows rose slightly. "He's buying."

"Impressive. Do you want to reschedule your appointment?"

She chuckled. "No. It's our first date. He won't be seeing any action that fast."

Stephen grinned. "I'm sure he'll be disappointed."

"I hope so." She pulled on a pair of white gloves. "I just saw your pretty wife. She's the one who did my hair. You're a lucky man to have caught her."

"I agree. Nora is very special."

"See that you remember that. She's been hurt too many times to survive another heartache at the hands of a man. Nora deserves someone who will love her and keep her safe for always." Her blue eyes turned knowing. "I think you might be him."

"I hope so," he said honestly, because Nora did deserve the best and he wasn't about to let her go so she could find that somewhere else.

"You probably know this already, but I'm going to tell you just in case." Myrna Nelson glanced around as if making sure they weren't about to be overheard. "Nora acts tough, but she has a very soft heart."

"I know. Have a good lunch, Myrna. I'll want details when I see you this afternoon."

She chuckled again. "But, Doctor, a lady never

kisses and tells." She gave him a quick wave and left.

Stephen stared after her, but he wasn't thinking about Myrna and her gentleman friend. Instead he was thinking about his softhearted wife and all the men who had hurt her. Was he going to be just one more in a long line? Had he made a mistake by insisting that they marry? In some ways he was as bad as David Fitzgerald. He didn't love her, either. At least he'd been honest from the first, telling her that he couldn't.

But what had seemed wise and reasonable a month ago no longer made sense. His deathbed promise to Courtney had been about trying to right a wrong. More guilt than true feeling. Did that mean he could let it go? Was he free to love someone else, and if so, did he want to love Nora?

He thought about being with her, living with her and enjoying every minute of their time together. What if he fell in love with her and then lost her, too? What about their baby? He couldn't survive the death of another child.

Then a voice in his head asked an uncomfortable question. Did he hold himself back because of Courtney, or because he was trying to keep himself safe?

He couldn't answer that by himself. He reached for the phone and dialed the number for the Snip 'n Clip. But Jill told him that Nora had gone home for lunch. Stephen thanked her and hung up, then rose to his feet and grabbed his keys. It was time he and his wife got this matter settled once and for all.

He walked into the small house ten minutes later. Nora wasn't in the living room or the kitchen. He called her name, then heard a loud *thunk* from the direction of the bedroom.

"Nora?"

He walked down the short hallway and into the bedroom. She stood with her back to him. His large suitcase was open on the bed and she was frantically tossing in clothes. *His clothes.*

He watched her in stunned silence. She was throwing him out? Just like that? No conversation, no questions. His chest tightened and his midsection tensed as if he'd taken a sharp, unexpected blow to the gut.

"What are you doing?"

She gasped, then spun toward him. That morning she'd pulled her long, dark hair into a French braid, so he could see all of her face. Her cheeks were wet with tears, her eyes and mouth swollen from crying.

She sniffed, then turned away, reaching for a pile of sweaters. His sweaters. "What does it look like. I'm helping you pack. If you're going back to Boston, you better get going." She walked to his dresser and scooped out an armful of socks. Instead of walking back to the bed, she simply threw them in that direction. Two or three pairs hit their target, but the rest fell on the floor. Nora didn't seem to notice.

"Boston?" Is that what she'd said? "How did you know about that?"

She glared at him. Fresh tears trailed down her face. "I knew it," she said, her voice low and defeated. She leaned against the dresser. "You were keeping it a secret. When did you plan to tell me? Before you left or after you were gone? If you were leaving, then why did you bother marrying me?" Her expression turned hostile. "Don't for a moment think you're getting custody of this baby. I'll do whatever

I have to in order to keep my child here, in Lone Star Canyon.''

He took a step toward her. ''Nora, I'm not going anywhere. The only thing I know about Boston is that I received a letter from someone I used to work with. He offered me a position running an emergency room. I haven't spoken with him or written back. But I intended to tell him I wasn't interested. I don't want to go anywhere. My life is here with you.''

''Don't expect me to believe that line of crap. If you meant it, you would have told me about the letter.''

''I just got it this morning. How did you find out about it?''

Her gaze narrowed, telling him he wasn't going to be able to talk his way out of this one easily. ''Some man left a message on the answering machine. Neil somebody. He said that he decided a letter wasn't good enough, so he was calling and wanted to know what it would take to get you back where you belonged.''

She brushed away the tears on her cheeks. Her shoulders rounded as if some of the fight had gone out of her. ''He's right, you know. You do belong there. You can't be happy here. The town is too small, there's nothing to do.'' She looked directly at him. ''Go home, Stephen.''

''I told you—I'm not leaving. I didn't have to make a decision. When I read Neil's letter, I wasn't the least bit tempted.''

''But you will be. It's just a matter of time.''

''How do you know that?''

''I just do.''

''No. You're wrong. This is everything I've ever

wanted. Emergency medicine was a mistake for me. I got sidetracked, but now I'm where I belong.''

She straightened. ''That sounds really good, but I don't believe it for a second. If Courtney was still alive, you'd still be in Boston.''

''That's because she wouldn't have wanted to live anywhere else.''

''It always comes back to her.'' Pain filled her eyes. ''I can't do this, Stephen. I should probably hang on longer, but I don't see the point. Nothing is going to change between us. You'll always be in love with her and I can't spend the rest of my life being second best. I don't want to wake up every morning and wonder if this is going to be the day you walk out on me just like every other man.''

''It's not like that.''

He moved toward her and reached out to touch her arm. She ducked out of range.

''I'm not them,'' he said, fighting frustration, not sure how to get through to her. ''I'm not going anywhere.''

''Why would I believe you? My father and David both claimed to love me and they left. You don't even have those feelings, so why would you stay? What's going to keep you here? The baby? For how long?''

''Dammit, why do you keep bringing up love? What do you want from me?''

She shook her head. ''The one thing I can't have. I realize I only have myself to blame. You gave me plenty of warning, but before I knew what had happened, I found that I'd fallen in love with you. I'd sworn I'd never do this again, yet here I am. But instead of being smart and falling for someone who would at least try to love me back, I picked you. Someone in love with another woman.''

He didn't know what to say. He couldn't think about anything but what she'd said. In love with him? Nora? When? How?

''I suppose it could be worse,'' she continued, ''although I'm not sure how. Because you're not just in love with any woman. You're in love with your wife, who died in childbirth. Courtney will always be young and perfect in your mind. I can't compete with a ghost and I don't want to.''

She brushed away her tears. ''I recognize that I'm an idiot. I won't ever have possession of your heart. I've set myself up for a life of unhappiness and I'm sorry we got married. We need to find another way to deal with the baby.''

''What are you saying?''

''I don't care if you're going to Boston or not. Either way, I want a divorce.''

Chapter Sixteen

Stephen couldn't believe they were actually having this conversation. He didn't know which shocked him more—the fact that Nora had said she wanted a divorce, or her confession that she loved him. He wanted to freeze them in place so he could have time to think about all that she'd said. He wanted to start at the beginning, back when they'd first met and do things differently...better. But most of all he wanted to gather her in his arms and hold her close while she told him again that she loved him.

Nora—the most beautiful, funny, honest woman he'd ever known. How on earth had he won her? And how could she tell him she loved him in one breath and then ask for a divorce in the second?

"Quit looking so happy," she told him, moving past him and heading down the hall.

"You love me," he said, trailing after her. "Why wouldn't I be pleased?"

"I guess you would. Typical man. Is that all you heard of our conversation? Parts of what I said were more important."

He caught up with her in the center of the kitchen. He touched her arm so that she turned to face him.

"I heard everything you said," he told her. "I don't want a divorce. I want to be with you. I'm not leaving Lone Star Canyon."

Her brown eyes flashed with temper. "I can't see where that makes a difference. What is the point of staying together? You're still in love with Courtney."

"We're having a child together. Nothing has changed for me. I want to be a part of my baby's life."

"I want to win the state lotto but I don't see that happening anytime soon. We all want things, but that doesn't mean they happen."

"This is going to happen. I'm not leaving," he repeated. "And I will be involved with the baby."

"Fine. Be involved. I still want a divorce."

Her words cut through him like a sword. He liked being married to Nora. He liked how she was feisty from the moment she woke up, and how she was so careful to separate the colors when she did laundry. He liked the sound of her laughter and her off-key singing in the shower. He liked the way she felt next to him in bed, just before they fell asleep. He liked knowing she was going to be there when he got home.

"Is there anything I can say to change your mind?" he asked.

A look of agony flashed across her face. For the first time he genuinely understood that he was hurting her. Then she blinked and her emotions were concealed behind an unreadable mask.

"I don't want to live half a life," she said. "If I'm going to be stupid enough to give my heart to a man, I want that man to love me back. You're not going to do that, so I want to be free to find someone who will."

"You'd marry someone else?" Outrage filled his words.

She looked at him as if he was as stupid as a rock. "Of course. What did you think? That I would spend my life pining for the likes of you? I'm weak, but I'm not insanely moronic. Why would I try to stay in love with someone who's determined not to return my feelings?"

He didn't have an answer to that, but he knew he didn't want her to go and he didn't want her with anyone else.

"I won't give you a divorce," he announced.

"I'm not surprised. However, this isn't the Middle Ages, oh great master. I don't need your permission."

She started walking out of the kitchen. At the doorway, she turned and looked at him. "The thing is, Stephen, you're wrong not to love me. Not just because I'm a hell of a catch, because I am, but because you're cheating yourself out of something very special. Hearts aren't meant to love just one person. They stretch and grow to accommodate any number of people. But you don't believe that."

"It's not that simple." Even to him the words sounded lame, but how was he supposed to explain about Courtney and his guilt?

"It should be. Even though I said I wouldn't go to Boston, I didn't really mean it. If you loved me back,

I would go anywhere with you." She leaned against the door frame, her dark eyes staring into his soul. "Are you going to love the baby?"

"Of course. How can you even ask?"

"It's surprisingly easy. What if I have twins? Can you love both children equally?"

Her question didn't make sense. "Of course."

"Why? You can't love two women but you're willing to love two children. What's the difference?"

He stared at her but couldn't answer.

"That's the point," she said, her voice soft now. "Which you didn't get at all. You assumed it was an either-or proposition, but it isn't. Yes, I want you to love me, but that has nothing to do with your feelings for Courtney. I think there's room for both of us, but you don't agree. I'm not going to waste my life trying to change your mind."

She headed for the front door. He hurried after her. "You can't just leave right in the middle of this."

"There's nothing more to say. Besides, I have clients waiting. I'd like you out of here by the time I get home."

And then she was gone.

Stephen stood at the front window and watched her drive away. He'd always known that Nora was gutsy, but he hadn't had a clue as to her inner strength. She wouldn't let him treat her badly, no matter how much she was in love with him. She would never be a victim.

He could only imagine how strong her child would be and the wonderful lessons he or she would be taught. Nora wasn't a quitter, but she wasn't a fool, either. She evaluated the situation, weighed the possibilities, then did what had to be done. Even if that meant facing the scandal of a divorce coming so quickly on the heels of a sudden marriage.

He walked into the bedroom and stared at his half-full suitcase. Clothes were scattered across the bed, with socks in a pile on the floor. Obviously her temper had gotten the best of her. Not that he could blame her. Hearing a message for him about a job in Boston would have set her off. That combined with her feelings and his insistence that Courtney always come first would have destroyed her.

Because he knew the truth about Nora. All her life she'd been second best to the wealthy Fiztgeralds. While she'd been growing up, the Darbys had been the poor family. Russell hadn't loved her enough to stay; David hadn't loved her enough to be true. She'd given up on men because she'd found them unworthy of her perfect, giving heart. Then he'd come along with his brilliant idea about an affair rather than true love. Maybe it would have worked or maybe it wouldn't have, but her getting pregnant had changed everything.

He moved into the small second bedroom. Several boxes of his stood in a corner. He hadn't unpacked them at his apartment and he'd only intended to store them here until they were settled in a larger house. He read the labels and found what he wanted in the third box from the bottom. He shifted the cartons until he could open that one. Inside were several mementos and photo albums from his past.

He picked up the wedding album and studied the pictures inside. Both he and Courtney looked young. He'd been so in love with her that day. He remembered how happy he'd been. He'd decided to give up his dream of being a small-town doctor and had changed to emergency medicine. He'd—

Stephen froze in the act of turning a page. He hadn't been happy about the change at all. He'd been angry and resentful. Courtney hadn't demanded or tried to coerce him, but she'd made her opinions known. If he wanted to go live in some town in the sticks, that was fine with her, but she wasn't going with him. Once he'd agreed to emergency medicine, she'd pushed him toward more prestigious hospitals, urging him to study with prominent doctors. She'd talked about what it would be like when they were both teaching as well as practicing. She'd been as concerned about the hierarchy of medicine as with the practice.

He thought about all the times she'd given up time with him to attend a cocktail party or a seminar. She'd worked hard for her fellowship, but she'd also ignored the toll it would take on her in terms of time and their relationship. It's not that he'd wanted her to change her dreams or work less, it's that he'd wanted her to realize there was more in the world than her career and his. After all, they'd had a marriage to nurture.

Or there had been. Stephen closed the album and realized that he'd been angry with Courtney for a long time before she died. His love had been fading a little each day, and the last of the flame had gone out when she'd talked about terminating her pregnancy. He hadn't loved her anymore when she'd passed away.

He hadn't loved her, so why had he made that damn promise? Why had he sworn never to love anyone else?

The truth echoed in his brain. An ugly truth that made him ashamed of himself. He'd promised not to love anyone else because he felt guilty for forcing Courtney to carry the baby to term. When the pregnancy had caused her death, he'd felt responsible. But it was more than that. He'd sworn his inappropriate oath because he was afraid. If he didn't love anyone else, he could never lose a piece of his heart again. Not feeling, not getting too involved meant not hurting. Because he'd not only had to mourn the death of his wife and his marriage, but the loss of his son.

He closed his eyes against the image of that tiny stillborn body. So perfect, yet so cold. A part of himself had died with his son. He hadn't been enough of a father to save him—even though he was a doctor and on the cutting edge of medicine. There were some things mortal man couldn't fix.

Pain and loss swirled inside of him. He wanted a second chance with his son. He wanted to hold that baby in his arms and somehow create a miracle that would allow him to breathe life into tiny lungs.

But there was no second chance. Only God could create a miracle. And perhaps He had. Another life…another chance…another baby.

Stephen had been holding himself back because he was afraid to connect and lose again. But what if it was different? What if this baby lived? Nora had asked if he would love his child and he'd said he would, but was that true? Would he open his heart to another infant, knowing there were no guarantees?

Pain filled him. Pain and hopelessness. He'd done everything wrong. He'd lost Courtney and his baby and now he'd lost Nora. She was going to leave him and marry someone else. Someone who loved her.

''I love her,'' he said as he shoved the photo album

back into the box. "I love her and I'm not letting her get away."

The words shocked him. He turned them over in his mind to see if they were correct. He felt more than heard the answer. There was a sense of rightness in his heart. A warmth flooded him as he thought about being with Nora, having children and a life with her, growing old with her. She was everything he'd ever wanted.

He knew then that he couldn't lose her. Whatever it took to convince her he would do. Because he'd finally figured out where he belonged—and that was at the side of his heart's desire.

Nora worked mechanically, grateful for the years of training that allowed her to continue to cut and style hair with sure fingers while inside her chest, her heart was slowly dissolving. She'd hoped she'd already been through the worst of the pain, but with each breath, the agony increased until she didn't know how she was going to survive without Stephen. How could she have told him that she wanted a divorce?

How could she have stayed with him, knowing that he didn't love her?

That's really what it came down to. The fact that he wasn't willing to love them both. She'd meant what she'd told him—she didn't have to be the only one in his heart. She could understand his need to love Courtney. They'd married, lived and grown together. They'd also been about to have a baby. If he would just make room for both of them. But he wasn't willing to meet her halfway so she had to protect her heart. If she stayed with him, loving him and knowing that he didn't love her back, she would start dying inside. Bit by bit, over time, until there was nothing left of her soul.

She couldn't do that to herself or to her child. She had to be alive and ready to take on the responsibilities of being a mother. However much she loved Stephen now, it would only get worse in time. Far better to cut him out of her life while she was still able.

Oh, but she was going to miss him. She'd loved being married to him. Even when he was driving her crazy, she didn't want to be with anyone else. No other man had ever taken the time to see past her prickly exterior. No one else would have understood that she was ambivalent about giving up her house. Not only had he understood, he'd given her all the time she needed.

She sprayed Debbie Watson's new haircut, then smiled at her in the mirror. "All finished."

"Thanks, Nora. You're gifted." But the thirty-something mother of four didn't move from her chair. "What's wrong?"

Nora touched her hand to her chest. "With me? Nothing."

Debbie didn't look convinced by her answer. "I would swear I just saw tears in your eyes. Are you all right?"

"I'm fine," Nora lied.

She knew that she couldn't keep her divorce from Stephen a secret very long, but she wanted to try. She'd been the subject of gossip enough times to know how unpleasant it was going to be. Her brief marriage and the supposed resulting pregnancy would only add fuel to the burning fire of the Nora Darby saga. After Stephen left her, she would be marked as a man-hater for sure.

The front door opened with a tinkle as the glass bumped the bell hanging just inside the door frame. She automatically glanced up. Her entire body went still when she saw Stephen standing there.

She hadn't thought he might follow her to continue their conversation. Didn't he know that there wasn't anything left to say? She opened her mouth to tell him that she was busy when something about his expression caught her attention. He looked shell-shocked, but also determined. And there was a light in his eyes that she'd never seen before. It made the hairs on the back of her neck stand up and her heart beat faster.

He looked around, spotted her, then headed directly for her station.

"Stop right there," she said, knowing she was an idiot for being glad to see him. She picked up a pair of scissors and held them out like a weapon. "I'm not afraid to use these."

To her surprise, he smiled. "I know. You're not afraid of anything, are you? I'm the one who's afraid, although I just figured that out."

He paused by Debbie's chair, although he didn't seem to notice the woman, nor the other interested bystanders in the salon.

"I didn't realize a lot of things," he continued. "I've been stupid and I'm sorry."

"Honey, you're a man. You can't help that," Mrs. Gelson piped up from her place at the dryers. She'd pushed back the hood so she could hear what was going on.

Stephen ignored her. "I have to talk to you," he

said, taking Nora's hand in his and tugging her toward the back of the salon.

If she'd been wearing heels she would have dug them into the linoleum to resist. "Stephen, I can't. I have customers."

"They can wait. This can't."

He pulled her into the shampooing area. She thought about pointing out that her office would be a better place to talk, but she wasn't in the mood to make anything especially easy for him. Besides, no one was at the bowls so they had a small amount of privacy. Not that he was likely to say anything she wanted to hear. She set her scissors on the counter and folded her arms over her chest.

"What do you want?"

Instead of answering, he pulled her close and kissed her. If she'd known what he was going to do she might have found the strength to resist him. Instead she melted into his embrace, savoring the scent and taste of the man she was going to love for the rest of her life. Passion, love and pain burned together in her heart. She'd meant it when she'd told Stephen she wanted a divorce, but she'd lied about finding someone else. She knew it was going to take a lifetime to recover from losing him.

"Stop," she whispered, pushing away from him.

"You don't want me to stop," he told her. "You want me to keep on being with you and loving you for the rest of our lives."

Her breath caught in her throat. She stared at him, at the light shining in his hazel eyes. He smiled.

"I love you," he said simply. "I have for a long time. I didn't recognize the symptoms because I didn't want to have to deal with my past. It was easier to tell myself that it was friendship and passion, not love. But I was wrong.''

He put his hands on her shoulders and squeezed. ''I don't want to go back to Boston. I don't care what the job is or even that you'd come with me—although I wouldn't go otherwise. But that's not the point. My life is *here*. In Lone Star Canyon. With you, Nora. Only with you. I want us to have our family here. I want to grow old here. I want our children's children to talk about old Doc Remington and wonder when I'm finally going to retire.''

She desperately wanted to believe him. Inside she was torn, needing to know that he loved her and wondering how it was possible. She searched his face, her fingers following the direction of her eyes as she touched his cheeks, his nose, his mouth.

''What about Courtney?'' she forced herself to ask.

Sadness crept into his eyes. ''She never wanted to get pregnant. At least not when she did. She had a fellowship and was working long hours. She wanted to terminate her pregnancy, but I convinced her otherwise. When I lost both her and the baby, I felt punished for being selfish. I was afraid to go through that again.''

He swallowed. ''At the risk of showing you that I have dark sides, too, my marriage to her was in trouble long before she got pregnant. But her resistance to having our child killed any lingering feelings. If she'd lived, we wouldn't have stayed together very long.''

His words washed over her like a soothing balm. Later she would find out the details and ask her questions, but for now it was enough to know that she wasn't going to have to compete with perfection.

"I felt responsible for all that had gone wrong," he continued. "She and the baby were both gone. The only way I knew to fix the past was to punish myself. I did that by swearing I would never love anyone again. Pretty dumb, huh?"

She smiled. "As Mrs. Gelson said before—you're a man. You can't help being a little thick."

He smiled, too. A slow, confident smile that spoke of love and a wonderful future. "Forgive me for being all the things I shouldn't have been. For being selfish and blind. You are the most amazing woman I've ever met. I'd be lost without you. I can't imagine anything more perfect than being married to you and having children with you. I love you with all my heart. I'll do anything if you'll just give me another chance. I thought I was marrying you to be close to my child and to keep you safe. I've realized I don't have any control over the future. I did the right thing for the wrong reason. Now I want to change that. I want us to stay married because we love each other. Tell me I'm not too late."

Her heart filled with joy, but she didn't give in to the urge to throw her arms around his neck and promise him the world. Instead she drew in a breath, determined to be as honest as he had been.

"I love you," she said. "I have for a long time. But before we make another commitment to each other, we need to make sure we understand each other." She hesitated. "You don't have to stay in Lone Star Canyon if you don't want to. I don't want to leave, but I will because I need you to be happy. But you have to understand this is who I am. I'll always be a hairdresser. I'm not going to college and getting a fancy degree just so you can tell your doctor friends that your wife is a lawyer or psychologist or something.''

He swept her up in his arms and spun her around the small room. ''I don't want you to change anything.'' He put her down and kissed her. ''I love *you*. Because you're a hairdresser and you give with your whole heart. Because you have more throw pillows in your house than I've ever seen in one place before. Because you're the smartest, sassiest woman I've ever met. Stay with me. Love me. Be my wife.''

Suddenly she was laughing and crying and holding him close and repeating the word ''Yes'' over and over. When she was silent, they gazed into each other's eyes.

It was only then she heard a faint sniffing sound. She shifted so she could look at the entrance to the small alcove. There stood her entire staff and every customer in the salon. Most of them were crying and smiling all at the same time.

Mrs. Gelson waved a lacy hankie. ''I never thought I'd live to see the day a man would scale Mount Nora and live to tell the tale.''

Epilogue

Exactly nine months to the day after the incident of the broken condom, Nora Darby Remington delivered a perfect, healthy baby girl. She was six pounds, ten ounces and nearly twenty inches long, and even the delivery nurse had to admit she was uncommonly beautiful.

That night Stephen stared up at the cold, clear January sky and saw the stars twinkling down at him. A sense of contentment, unlike any he'd ever known, filled him. His wife and daughter were sleeping peacefully. Tomorrow they would all go home to their new house and begin their life as a family.

He knew he'd been very lucky to get a second chance at love. Especially with a woman like Nora. She knew him as well as he knew himself... sometimes she knew him better. Over the past few months he'd talked about his life with Courtney, explaining what had gone right and wrong. They'd vowed to always talk about what was bothering them, even when throwing dishes seemed so much easier. She'd held him when he'd ached for the loss of a tiny baby boy. And she'd helped him heal.

A tree stood in their backyard. It wasn't very big now, but in time it would grow to touch the sky. A small brass plaque dedicated the tree in the name of a child who had never seen the sky or felt the warmth of the sun. It had been Nora's idea.

All the best ones were.

* * * * *

*Don't miss the next
book in Susan Mallery's*
LONE STAR CANYON *miniseries,*

WIFE IN DISGUISE.

*Coming to you from
Silhouette Special Edition
in March 2001.*

ATTENTION
LINDSAY McKENNA FANS!

Morgan's men are made for battle—
but are they ready for love?

Coming in February 2001:

MAN WITH A MISSION
(Silhouette Special Edition #1376)

Featuring rugged army ranger Jake Travers as
he comes under the captivating command of
beautiful Captain Ana Lucia Cortina.

*And available in March 2001,
a brand-new, longer-length single title:*

Morgan's Mercenaries:
Heart of Stone

Featuring Captain Maya Stevenson as she is reunited
with Major Dane York—her powerful enemy
turned passionate lover!

And in April 2001, look for a special collection
featuring the stories that started it all—
Morgan's Mercenaries: *In the Beginning....*

Available at your favorite retail outlet.

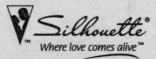

Where love comes alive™

#1 *New York Times* bestselling author

NORA ROBERTS

brings you more of the loyal and loving,
tempestuous and tantalizing Stanislaski family.

Coming in February 2001

The Stanislaski Sisters

Natasha and Rachel

Though raised in the Old World traditions of their
family, fiery Natasha Stanislaski and cool, classy
Rachel Stanislaski are ready for a *new* world of love....

*And also available in February 2001 from
Silhouette Special Edition, the newest book in the
heartwarming Stanislaski saga*

CONSIDERING KATE

Natasha and Spencer Kimball's daughter Kate turns her
back on old dreams and returns to her hometown, where
she finds the *man* of her dreams.

Available at your favorite retail outlet.

Where love comes alive™

Silhouette invites you to come
back to Whitehorn, Montana...

MONTANA MAVERICKS

WED IN WHITEHORN—
12 BRAND-NEW stories that capture living
and loving beneath the Big Sky where legends
live on and love lasts forever!

MM

And the adventure continues...

February 2001—
Jennifer Mikels *Rich, Rugged...Ruthless* (#9)

March 2001—
Cheryl St.John *The Magnificent Seven* (#10)

April 2001—
Laurie Paige *Outlaw Marriage* (#11)

May 2001—
Linda Turner *Nighthawk's Child* (#12)

Available at your favorite retail outlet.

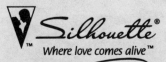

In March 2001,

Silhouette Desire

presents the next book in

DIANA PALMER's

enthralling *Soldiers of Fortune* trilogy:

THE WINTER SOLDIER

Cy Parks had a reputation around Jacobsville for his taciturn and solitary ways. But spirited Lisa Monroe wasn't put off by the mesmerizing mercenary, and drove him to distraction with her sweetly tantalizing kisses. Though he'd never admit it, Cy was getting mighty possessive of the enchanting woman who needed the type of safeguarding only he could provide. But who would protect the beguiling beauty from *him…?*

Soldiers of Fortune…prisoners of love.

Silhouette®
Where love comes alive™

*Available only from
Silhouette Desire at
your favorite retail outlet.*

Visit Silhouette at
www.eHarlequin.com

SDWS

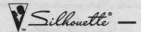

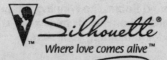